MURDER IN THE MINE

A gripping crime mystery full of twists

ROY LEWIS

JOFFE BOOKS

Revised edition 2019 by Joffe Books, London.

First published as "A Question of Degree" in 1974

www.joffebooks.com

ISBN-13: 978-1-78931-071-9

Please note this book is set in the early 70s in England, a time before mobile phones and DNA testing, when social attitudes were very different.

CHAPTER 1

The mountain drew him.

Blankets of rain cloud obscured the upper valley, and in the darkness the lean, emaciated trees behind the street dripped in a contemplative misery. As he walked up the track that had once rumbled to countless coal trucks the dirt rasped under his shoes. No traces of the old lines now remained; where they had been, a rivulet now ran, trickling down the hill to the village.

The wind was light on his wet face and the mountain was silent. He reached the brow of the hill and stopped, looked back behind him. Just below were the street lights of Pentre, curling away down to Ton and then ribboning away towards Dinas and Tonypandy. But the rain would soon shroud those lights. He turned and the dark shape of the old pit head loomed up ahead of him. Against the blackness of the hill he could just make out the winding house and the ruined buildings that had once been offices. They stood there in the wet night like so many sentinels guarding the corridors of the past, but it was not the ancient past that bothered him, it was the recent past, two months . . . it seemed like years.

He walked past the winding house, stumbling over loose brick and iron, and the manager's office was to his left, ruined and broken-down. The wheelhouse lay ahead of him and it was as though it exerted some magnetic pull, drawing him towards it as it had done several times during these last months.

The entrance was black and menacing but he went in. Moisture dripped slowly through the broken roof. It was darker in here, too dark to see anything tonight. But he could remember.

The wheelhouse was silent yet full of echoes for him: echoes of the past, long dead echoes, overlaid by the taunting, threatening tones of a woman he thought he would never see again. He was unable to escape from her voice and her words. They came back to him in the small hours in his own home as they came back now, the words and the anger.

And the violence.

He could hardly remember what it was like, that violence. He had never struck anyone before, never a blow. But she had taunted him, and the taunts were in a sense worse than her threats and her demands for they tore into his emotions like claws into raw flesh. It was not the woman he had struck out against, but the words; it had been a defensive action born of anger and despair and hate of this woman who had come back out of the past.

And since then, silence. Long nights, painful days, the mountain looming up, the wheelhouse and the shaft, the scene of the quarrel, up here waiting, and the silence grew and lengthened and perhaps it would always be so.

A long silence.

He hoped it would be so; he prayed it would remain that way. A long silence. He stood there and the rain began in earnest. He waited a little while, in the darkness, but the voices were in his head, and he walked back down the track and went home.

On the mountainside, apart from the wind and the rain and the little scurrying animals, there was only the dead silence of darkness.

* * *

When Dai Chippo had come out of the Army he had a few tales to tell, a gratuity in the bank, a Scottish wife with a tongue as sharp as her parsimony, and the vague idea he'd like to set up in business. The only place available was the house on top of Pentre hill, right next door to a decaying entrance to a timber merchant (retired) and opposite the crumbling walls beyond which the old tram tracks, now greened over with disuse, ran steeply up the mountainside to the pit head, closed down this twenty years.

It was a good place for a business nevertheless, for it was near the Red Lion, which discharged men seeking penitent fish-and-chip suppers for their deserted wives, and only one hundred yards from the Conservative Club where committed Labour Party card-holders, who somehow reasoned they were bleeding the Conservatives white by playing billiards there all day and drinking subsidised beer, emerged at lunchtime for a quick snack. And on the hill there was no competition for Dai Chippo: the only business premises were the drapery stores at the bottom and the estate agents across the road.

The image of being a fish-fryer's wife had not appealed to his wife Margaret but she had given in and Dai had had no regrets — there had been one bad patch when in the interests of profits and economy he had been reckless and Joe Joseph Weights-and-Measures had smelled a rat, found one, and then discovered in addition that Dai was using pig potatoes. But it had all blown over, especially when Dai had started selling other lines such as steak and kidney pies and chicken breasts. Faggots didn't go.

He liked the job. Some nights, when the rain mists gathered at the top of the valley, hovering over Rhigos, sending wet blanketing curtains into the valley and causing old miners to cough in the darkness, Dai used to put on his coat over his white shop jacket and hurry up to the church just for the pleasure of looking back at the bright neon sign: *FISH AND CHIPS*.

Nothing more than that. Functional. Dai Davies. *FISH AND CHIPS*. Dai Chippo. Margaret hated the sobriquet but Dai didn't mind it. Showed he was well known and liked. He enjoyed being liked. And he enjoyed his shop.

People came in and talked. Old people, youngsters, kids, men and women, they came in for a bag of chips and a chicken leg and they stayed on to talk. Most of the gossip from the Rhondda came into his shop. And most of the people from Pentre. Dai liked people. Especially women. He told them so, with his sly talk in the shop, and more directly on Tuesday afternoons when the shop was shut and Margaret was down at Ponty market with Mrs O'Connor, and other husbands were working day shift at the only pit left open or in the factories at Dinas Mawr or the Trading Estate.

Some Tuesdays he played billiards at the Club, or took Gyp for a walk.

* * *

'Found him yet, then?'

Dai watched his sallow-faced assistant, a Margaret appointment, all narrow face, thin chest, as much sex appeal as a Co-op wardrobe, and when she had scooped up and bagged the chips he took it from her and the package to Mrs Daniels.

'No, haven't seen hide nor hair of him, best part of a week. Little bugger.'

'Done it before, hasn't he?'

'Reg'lar.'

Dai turned to smile at the young woman who had just entered the shop; she had bold eyes, false eyelashes, and a smile as easy as her virtue. He grinned, widening and hardening the smile as he showed her his appreciation. He continued his conversation with Mrs Daniels but he looked at the young woman.

'Aye, he's done it regular, like, every time he gets the urge, you see. One thing you can say about dogs, Mrs Daniels, when they feel like it they do it. Whether it's cocking a leg against a tree or lifting it over a bitch they just get on and do it.'

Mrs Daniels giggled. 'There's coarse you are.'

'True enough, isn't that so?' Dai said, addressing the young woman. She raised a rigid, painted brow, affecting indifference.

'I wouldn't know. What's the chicken breasts like?'

'Chicken breast, woman's breast,' Dai chuckled softly. 'Beautiful . . . We're talking about my dog, you know, Gyp.'

'Not been around for a week,' Mrs Daniels said.

'Saw him across the road last Saturday morning,' the young woman said. 'I'll have six and two breasts if—'

'Across the road?'

'Aye, that's right. Trotting up where the trams used to run.'

Dai was puzzled. 'Gyp? Going up towards the Bwylffa? On a *Saturday?*'

'That's right. Morning.' She preened herself at the attention she was getting' 'Two breasts, I said, because Jim's home tonight and—'

'But he couldn't be,' Dai said positively.

Pained eyebrows shot up like twin drawbridges of surprise. 'Don't be so bloody soft. I know when my husband's home, don't I?' The lashes slammed down suddenly, aware of Mrs Daniels's inquisitive glance. 'Of course Jim's home.'

‘Not Jim,’ Dai said, flustering the young woman in a way he never flustered her on Tuesdays. ‘Gyp. He couldn’t have been going up the Bwylffa, not on a Saturday morning. If he had, he’d have come home for dinner. You’re wrong, Jean.’

You’re wrong, Dai, the bold angry eyes told him; if you want to come around next Tuesday you’d better admit it, too.

‘He’s my dog,’ Dai Chippo said stubbornly.

* * *

‘You’re not going up there in the rain to look for the dog, surely!’ Margaret said with the angry, snappish resignation of a righteous woman wronged.

‘Shop’s closed’ Dai said.

‘The way you carried on last night in bed,’ Margaret complained, ‘tossing and turning, talking in your sleep . . .’

‘Worried.’

‘You never worry like that about me!’

‘Gyp’s a dumb animal.’

Margaret flared, her pale eyes narrowing as she calculated, checking to discover from her husband’s countenance whether the remark carried a deliberate slight, but Dai Chippo’s face was expressionless as he reached for his raincoat.

‘Won’t be long,’ he said, and she let him go.

Dai closed the door quietly behind him. A car came rushing along the street, dipping into the hill, and spray lifted from its bonnet, causing Dai to pause as he crossed the road. There were few people about and it was one of those grey wet afternoons when a man was best leaning on a billiards table or sleeping with another man’s wife. He could make out the dim form of Martin Evans through the frosted glass of the estate agent’s office, Morgan and Enoch, but Dai did not pause to talk. He walked straight along the pavement towards the crumbling wall, clambered over the broken stone to the slope where the old rails had run and began to climb.

The old roadway ran directly up the mountainside admitting no curves, no weakness. Some of the old timbers were still there though the rails themselves were as long gone as their users. Dai's father had been a roadman in the pit, working in the blackness towards the face. He hadn't wanted Dai down there though Dai had been built for it: short, powerfully muscled shoulders, stocky in build.

Dai hadn't got his Higher School Certificate though, so he'd gone to the Army. Done well, he had. The old man said so with his eyes, before he died. He couldn't speak; pneumoconiosis and a series of strokes had stilled his tongue. Dai wished the old man had said it aloud, even so, just once while he had been alive. He never had. Dai had seen little affection from the old man.

Gyp, now, he wore his heart where everyone could see it. That was why Dai loved him. You knew where you were with Gyp.

The mist was down, wet and clinging, and there was little to be seen. The valley itself was all but hidden, only the top terraces emerging from the rain as Dai climbed. A sheep coughed somewhere across on the left, an old man's cough, harsh and gritty, and it reminded Dai of Ben Williams, the farmer. He stood no nonsense with dogs, if they came near his sheep he used his shotgun first and asked no questions then or later. A few dogs had disappeared on the mountain but no one had ever asked Ben about it down in the pub for he had a red eye.

* * *

He wouldn't have shot Gyp. The dog didn't bother sheep. Rabbits, yes, and there were a few coming back on the hill. But rats, mainly — it was why Dai had managed to persuade Margaret they needed a dog in the first place. Keep the rats out of the shop. Bound to come down from the old pit otherwise.

Ben Williams wouldn't have shot Gyp.

Dai stood beside the fence, peering across the wire towards the huddle of stone buildings that was the farm, as though seeking the information, wordlessly. Nothing moved around the farmyard; it lay as though deserted, and dispirited, Dai moved away.

Rats. Gyp loved rats as a hunter loves a quarry. He broke their back with a snap and a swing of his head. He was a bloody good dog. He'd have come up here, Saturday morning, looking for rats if he had come at all.

To the Bwylffa.

The ribs of the old wheelhouse loomed out of the mist as Dai crossed the old road that ran up from Pentre hill and down to Ton, passable still but never used now. The rusted boilers with their shattered pressure gauges lay clumped under the hill: Dai had seen kids playing submarines in those, coming out encrusted in red rust. The manager's office was a ruin now, roof gone, walls broken down, windows gaping like a toothless widow. Dai shivered. There was Death in this place and its damp hand touched his bones.

The trees dripped slowly, watchfully.

Dai walked across to the wheelhouse.

'Gyp!'

Echoes roared their surprise at him and then faded reedily, mumbling in discontent, only to shout back crazily again, a broken pattern of confused sound, when he tried again.

'Gyp! Where are you, boy?'

The wheelhouse yawned at him, the boilers watched him balefully, thirty years out of their time. They had earned their sleep. They seemed to resent his presence and the noise he was making.

'Gyp!'

It must have been the malignant echoes, sharpened, attuned to his imagination. Dai stood still quiet and careful as the crouching trees, and he listened. The echoes had gone and he waited.

Until it came.

* * *

Dai was surprised at his own lack of excitement. He waited again, listening hard, and then he moved hesitantly towards the wheelhouse. He called the dog's name again, heard the faint sound after the echoes had thrashed away their anger, and then he hurried forward towards the wheelhouse.

The timber spat at him with a cracking, rotten sound and he stopped in the doorway. Beyond, behind the bars and the chain, was the timbered entrance to the shaft. Sleepers had closed it but the years had opened it again. He could see the split between the rotten timbers and he thrust his way under the chain, past the bars and the leaning iron posts.

The rain grew stronger, spattering his hair and trickling down his neck as Dai got down on his knees on the green timber, leaned forward towards the broken, split shaft cover and he shouted again, with all the strength his lungs could offer.

'Gyp!'

The sound spiralled down a shaft deep and black as death but the whine that came up raised no hackles on Dai's neck, for it was a call for help.

Gyp was down in the shaft.

Dai ran all the way back to the police station.

* * *

'Difficult,' said the police sergeant.

'Bloody difficult,' said the man from the NCB.

'Been closed too long,' the mine surveyor said. 'Several falls, there's been, blocking up the shaft, but no telling whether it would take a man's weight. Dog, yes, but a man, I don't know about that.'

The cover had been removed, the rain had stopped, it was almost dark and the shaft was black and menacing.

'We'll have to get him up,' Dai said. 'He's been down there a week. He'll be starving.'

'Amazin' he's still alive,' the mine surveyor said. 'But there you are. Tough animals, dogs.'

'So how do we get him up?' Dai demanded impatiently.

The surveyor looked at him with an impassive eye. He was fond of pigeons himself. 'Can't use the ladder. Rusted away. Winch a chap down, in harness. Dicey, though, you know; sides could fall in if you're not careful. But we'll get the tackle rigged up, take us couple of hours. Then a man to go down with a lamp, trouble is if the dog's injured he might be vicious—'

'I'll go down,' Dai said.

'Aye, thought so.'

Floodlights were brought and the old wheelhouse gained new life as it lay bathed in the glow and was surrounded by busy men setting up the winching apparatus. The old timbers were torn away from the mouth of the shaft and the winch placed in position, the bucket and harness slung below it.

Dai had gone home and was now dressed in jeans and black sweater, albeit showered with invective from Margaret who thought grown men should not make so much fuss about a mere mongrel dog. The mine surveyor suggested Dai should wear a helmet, both for protection and for the light its lamp would afford in the blackness of the shaft. Dai accepted it readily enough.

The thought of entering the shaft was not an entertaining one.

He climbed into the bucket, strapped on the harness and with a shout he was swung into the shaft. The winch ground away above his head and the direct light from the floodlights was gone immediately, to be replaced only by a soft glow that played about the mouth of the shaft twenty feet above his head. Dai looked up and saw the rusted ladder rails reaching up to the surface and myriad points of light — drops of water — gleamed at him. Then he was dropping inch by inch into the shaft, the light seemed suddenly distant, and he became aware of the cold and the dampness all around him.

He switched on the lamp and the light pierced the gloom, so that he could see the runnels of water on the brick sides of the old shaft. He felt the bucket jar against the sides, swinging violently as he turned to look about him and down, and seemingly far below he caught sight of the blockage near the first level. The signal wire was in his left hand — there had not been time to rig up any wireless contact — and he pulled it twice, the prearranged signal. The bucket slowed in its descent, crawled, almost stopped. Dai leaned out of the bucket.

'Gyp?'

The whining sound that came back was clear enough. The dog was there all right, alive, probably starving, but below him on the rock fall. The bucket winched him down slowly and he turned his head, playing the lamp on the level.

Timber supports from the roof had collapsed, falling outwards and blocking the main shaft, or part of it at least. Dirt and rubble had accumulated there so that Dai could not have gone lower than the first level in any case. But he did not need to; Gyp, in his scurry after rats, had fallen through the boarding over the shaft and must have landed on the dirt — miraculously not killing himself in the process. The lamp shone into the entrance of the tunnel as he came lower and he caught the gleam of Gyp's eyes.

The dog was lying on its side, weakly, but it tried to rise as Dai came close. Its leg was broken; the sole incident of the fall, it would seem.

'Damned lucky' Dai said aloud, and in relief then tugged three times at the signal line. The bucket swayed, slowed, stopped, and Dai was just three feet above the level.

He stayed there for a few minutes, considering. Gyp could not come to him. He would have to get out of the bucket to reach him, but there was the chance the rubble below him would not bear his weight. The remains of the rusted girders where the cage had run were the main support but they were old and unreliable: nevertheless, there was no other way to do it.

Gingerly, Dai hoisted himself from the bucket, let it take his weight as he sought the ledge with his foot, and then continued to cling to it as he tested the platform of rubble. It seemed firm enough, sloping slightly down towards the entrance to the level. Keeping hold of the bucket he stepped away in careful fashion and then, emboldened, he released his hold and took two paces into the level.

Gyp was there at his feet, weak, licking his hand as he leaned over and caressed him.

'All right, boy, two minutes and we'll have you out.'

Dai explored the animal's body heard the whining growl when he touched the broken front leg, and then he levered the little body up into his arms.

'Right, boy, back into the bucket.'

He turned with Gyp and the lamplight flashed on something lying near the place where the dog's body had been. Dai paused, then turned away and reached for the bucket, placed the whimpering dog inside. He stood staring at Gyp for a moment then he turned back to the level.

The brooch gleamed at him in the darkness, bright as a jewel. It was in the form of an oval, speared by a jagged lightning bolt. Dai crouched, picked it up and looked at it while images flickered through his mind like an old, badly run film. At last, slowly, reluctantly he raised his head, directed the beam a few feet further into the tunnel.

With Dai and Gyp aboard, the bucket went for the surface in a series of smooth pulls, jerking them up faster than Dai had come down. When they finally emerged there was a light, ragged cheer from the half-dozen men gathered near the shaft entrance. Dai was assisted from the bucket. He carried Gyp in his arms like a baby. He was sweating profusely.

'Bloody good show,' the man from the NCB said, relieved that it had all gone without a hitch and without the need to pay compensation to anyone.

The mine surveyor put out a hand and tentatively touched Gyp's head. Pigeons didn't bite, but dogs did.

'He looks fit enough, really, for a week underground. Didn't starve, anyway.'

'No, he didn't starve,' Dai said and looked at the brooch in his left hand.

'What do you . . .' the mine surveyor began but the words died at the sight of Dai's face.

'He wasn't alone down there,' Dai said. It was only then that his teeth began to chatter.

* * *

The Bwylffa had seen nothing like it in the old days. Forty years ago there had been the bustle of men and horses and trams, the whistle of steam in the boilers and the hum and thump of the fan driving air down the shaft to the levels below. That had all gone now, and the years had quietened the pit head, twenty years of rust and grass had changed the character of the area, and there were only the rats and the foxes and the grass snakes to inhabit the hill.

Until the mongrel had fallen down the shaft.

Lights glared whitely down on the wheelhouse and the open shaft, there was a constant coming and going, vans and trailing cables and television equipment littered the pit head and across the stream, clusters of sightseers carried out vigils unlike those that had gone before in ancient pit disasters. Screens had been erected around the entrance to the shaft so the cameras were unable to obtain the kind of shots their handlers would dearly have loved to obtain but the skeletal steel of the wheelhouse and the lowering backdrop of the dark mountainside was some compensation; it gave the reporters the macabre atmosphere they desired to frame their story of mystery and death. It all helped to produce a frisson in the viewer, and that was good television. The presenter's tone was earnest.

'No details have yet been released and we have been unable to obtain comments from the senior police officers at the scene but considerable speculation has been aroused as to what exactly is to be found in the shaft. The story began in the late evening of yesterday when attempts were made to rescue a small dog that had been trapped in the old mine shaft. Its owner, Mr Davies, a local shopkeeper, was lowered into the shaft and was able to rescue the animal, but in so doing he discovered some items of clothing that excited his interest and suspicion.

A report was immediately made to the local police and the CID ordered the area to be sealed off and a further investigation made. Excitement here mounts now as increased activity at the wheelhouse leads us to believe that the investigation of the shaft, bedevilled as it has been by two further falls of a minor nature, reaches a climax. Informed sources tell us that there is a body in the shaft; that it is the body of a woman; that it has been in the shaft for some considerable time.'

'Was it you who spoke to the press, Dai?'

Dai Chippo looked around him, uncertainly. It was not that he was frightened by police stations, it was just he didn't like them. They were like dentists' surgeries: they made him feel anxious and vaguely uncomfortable.

And Detective-Inspector Dewi Jones had the same effect on him, too.

He knew all about Dewi Jones. A big man, built like a warship: a pugnacious head with a prow of a nose; broad in the beam, ponderous under full steam, but as effective and dangerous in his job as he had been in the boxing ring. Dai had seen him fight when he had been Mid-Rhondda champion, and though he had never seen Dewi when he became Police Area Champion at middleweight he had heard that Dewi was dynamite. And there were a few chaps in the valleys who knew about that too, outside the ring at that.

But speaking to the Press, what was wrong with that?

'No law against it, is there?'

'No law at all. But we'd have preferred you not to.'

Dai Chippo reassumed his smiling expression, even if he was still uncomfortably aware of the sweat in his armpits and on his forehead.

'It's been three days,' he said. 'I'm a businessman and these newspaper boys have been fussing around my shop all the damn time. Got on Margaret's nerves they have, and that means she has a go at me, you know?'

Dewi Jones knew. It was common knowledge that Margaret Davies put the fear of God in her husband, who thought she *was* God.

'And they keep asking for information, so what could I do? My wife on one shoulder, the Press on the other; all right, they brought in a bit of custom because even newsmen have to eat and fish and chips is as good as anything, but they lost me some too, thronging the shop. So I told them, explained to them what I knew about it all. I told them, just to bloody well get rid of them.'

'You told them all you knew?'

'Well, aye.'

'Is that more or less than you told us?'

There was a sadness in Dewi Jones's eyes that suggested he was well aware of the powers Pressmen had to extort information the police could not. Dai was nettled at the suggestion, however.

'I told it same as I told you.'

'Which was . . . what?'

'You've got it all down!'

'But tell me again, will you? Just to be on the safe side, like, so we know we've made no mistakes.'

Angrily, under no illusions, Dai told the detective inspector again. He sat and talked and watched Dewi's pen travel over the paper, writing in neat shorthand the words Dai used. Those words would be checked later against what Dai had said previously, so Dai kept strictly to his story. He told him about the descent and the rescue of the mongrel, Gyp; he told him about the light shining on the brooch, and then on what seemed a pile of old rags. He had picked up the brooch, looked more closely at the 'rags' and realised what he had found. He had felt sick and shaky. He had reported his find immediately upon reaching the surface. The police had come, taking their time as usual, the body had been brought to the surface.

'How did you know it was a woman, Dai?'

'Oh, come on, by her clothes, of course. And boyos don't wear brooches, do they?'

'How long do you think she'd been there?'

'Oh, about . . . hell, why ask me that? How should I know?'

Dewi Jones raised his eyebrows and glanced thoughtfully at the shopkeeper. 'Just a question, Dai. Don't get excited. I just wondered whether you'd told us all you know.'

'Nothing else to tell.'

Detective Inspector Jones tapped his pen against his teeth and stared at his notes. 'You sure, Dai? Tell you why I ask. When a chap's a copper like me, he gets to rely not just on facts and words and direct evidence. He relies a bit on impressions, too. He looks at the man he's interviewing and he begins to get an idea about what's making the man tick, you know? I don't know what's making you tick, Dai, but you're ticking all right. You're ticking scared.'

Dai Davies shook his head, nettled.

'What makes you think I'm scared? I got nothing to be scared about. I just found that body, by accident.'

'You've been sweating hard ever since you came in here, Dai, and your eye rolls around like a wall-eyed pit pony with the shakes. What's the trouble? You can tell me.'

Dai snorted. 'Tell you what? About the Pressmen who been charging all around my shop? About the women who'll talk a penn'orth of chips at the end of it? About the traipsin' up and down, up and down to the station here?'

'There's more than that, Dai,' Dewi Jones said quietly.

'You're damn right there's more! I was down in that bloody hole! I was fetchin' my dog and I saw that . . . that *thing* there. I tell you, it turned my stomach! And I can still see it, when I go to bed! It's all very well for chaps like you to talk but I saw it, I *touched* it!'

'I've seen and handled a few in my time too,' Jones said, a little stiffly. 'Headless bodies even, suicides on the tram lines down from the pit.'

'Aye, but you get bloody well paid to do it!'

Dewi Jones studied his notes, keeping his temper. He allowed the temperature to cool between them; he was still not entirely convinced; something bothered him about Dai Chippo's story, but it all stood up, and accorded well with what he'd been saying all along. 'So you got nothing more you want to add, then?'

* * *

'It's not much to go on, is it?' the Chief Superintendent said as he sat in conference with his senior CID staff.

'And the trail's pretty cold, too,' the Chief Constable added, not willing to remain completely silent.

'Three months, the pathologists reckon,' the liaison officer confirmed. 'When I was at the lab this morning they hadn't got very far even now. Couple of bones missing, after the second and third falls, maybe a couple disturbed—'

'Dai Chippo's dog.'

'Aye, I suppose . . .'

'And it's been all but a week,' the Chief Super said as he looked around. 'What do you think, sir?'

The Chief Constable shrugged. 'If you ask me, we need expert assistance.'

'The Mets?'

'Got no other choice, if you ask me. We'll have to foot expenses, of course.' The Chief Constable looked thoughtful, stroked his heavy jowls. 'We'll supply support staff and I'll sound out the Home Office about the whole thing. I'd like to feel we would be able to handle the investigation . . . *control* it if you know what I mean.'

The Chief Superintendent was doubtful 'Not usual, sir. I mean, if Scotland Yard send one of their men down he'll want full control. They always do.'

'Ah, yes, but this is a bit different. In the valleys they're a pretty close lot, you know that as well as I do. They'd clam up to someone from outside and he wouldn't get anywhere. So I think it needs to be seen that the Murder Squad man acts in an *advisory* capacity, a *consultative* capacity. If I make out the case to London they'll wear it, I'm sure, and the action will then be under our control.'

'And the policy decisions?'

'Those too.'

The Chief Superintendent looked around at the senior officers attending. They needed the assistance of the Murder Squad, but he couldn't see them sending a man who'd be prepared to play second fiddle.

'I'd like to think we *could* do it, sir.'

'We'll make out a case,' the Chief Constable said with more confidence than he really felt.

'Wales is different.'

'Something like that. We want someone from the Murder Squad but valley people being what they are, inbred, close-mouthed, I'll lay it on thick. . .We'll give it a try. Emphasise Murder squad . . . but advisory . . . consultative . . .'

CHAPTER 2

John Crow didn't like it. He had told Commander Bill Gray, quietly and succinctly, just what he thought of the proposition. Gray, the diplomat as ever, hadn't seen it in quite the same light as Crow.

'I consider you're regarding it in too severe a manner, John. I agree the request is unusual, but the Home Office see this as basically no different from sending another expert — such as someone from the Fraud Squad — to act as adviser. There are precedents for it. A rational request—'

'I've already made my point. The arguments they raise look good on paper. They won't work in theory. You know as well as I that an investigation must be the responsibility of one man, ultimately. And that man must be the senior investigating officer.'

'I don't see your problem,' Gray said blandly. 'You'll be the investigating officer in all but name. You'll be designated as acting in an advisory capacity but you'll be working in precisely the same way as you always work—'

'Except that I'll be giving *advice*, which someone else—'

'The Chief Constable.'

'- can accept or reject. It won't work.'

'Not unless it's tried. And you will try it, won't you, John?'

'If ordered to do so,' Crow said stiffly. 'Under protest.'

Gray smiled and pressed a button on his desk. 'That's all right then,' he said.

* * *

It was not the best day on which to make his first acquaintance with the Rhondda. The afternoon had started brightly enough and the sun had still been shining over Bristol when the train had pulled out of Templemeads Station, but by the time it reached Cardiff the clouds had drawn over and the rain began as the police car took him out through Llandaff towards the Rhondda.

'You ought to try to get to see Llandaff Cathedral while you're down here,' the police driver said affably. 'Worth a visit, sir.'

The valley, Crow thought, was definitely not worth a visit. The drive out of Cardiff was pleasant enough in spite of the rain, but after they passed the narrow streets of Pontypridd he saw the blackness of the mean river and the scruffiness of the stone-littered hillside and his heart dropped. He was not looking forward to the assignment — not that he looked forward to any of them, but this less than most — and the way in which the mountains began to crowd in on him as he proceeded up the valley began to induce a feeling of acute depression. He felt hemmed in, physically and emotionally, by the valley and the job.

Headquarters had been established at Tonypandy but the police driver quickly explained that a room had been taken for him in a hotel in Cardiff.

'Nothing decent up around here, you see, sir. Thing is, there's a few commercial travellers and they use the pub but in the main there's no real hotels you could use—a couple in Ponty perhaps, but we're so close to Cardiff you'd just as well stay there.'

The Chief Constable said much the same thing after he introduced Crow to the team with which he would be working.

'It was that or Caerphilly. We thought it would be useful if you came up here first, got introduced and all that, and then after you've had a chance to ask the questions you want to ask we'll lay on a car and take you back to Cardiff.'

'I would really have preferred to stay in the valley,' Crow replied, much against his inclinations. It was not that he preferred the valley so much as his being placed in Cardiff suggested he was being located at one remove from the centre of operations. 'Emergencies can arise, and it's likely I will be working until late on occasions. Is there no place. . .'

'I think not,' the Chief Constable said. His eyes were blank, regarding the suggestion as an unwelcome one. 'Nothing suitable. You'll be better off in Cardiff. A car will be made available to you. No trouble.'

No one else spoke. Crow looked around him and sensed a certain hostility. It was not new to him. Many local officers resented the intrusion of the Murder Squad; it was like saying the local detectives were not good enough to do the job. It was often an unpopular decision. But that was none of his business. It was local politics. He had to work with these people; in time their reserve and closeness might disappear. He nodded his head.

'All right. I'll accept your advice. Now my brief—'

'We discussed it at length with the Home Office,' the Chief Constable said brusquely, but smiling a false smile. 'We've thought that in the circumstances we'd like to *use* you, drain you dry, if you like, ha, ha! We're in a difficult position, you see. Our local force could probably handle matters, but the time element is against us. And your expertise and experience will be useful. But valley people are funny people, and I speak as one who knows them. It's a close, inbred community. It doesn't take kindly to outsiders — and even a Cardiff man is an outsider. It's true many people work in Cardiff, commute to and from the valley — but the Rhondda is self-sufficient. And a Murder Squad man, well, you can imagine, can't you?'

'Might get less than co-operation,' Crow said quietly. 'I understand the position perfectly.'

His tone also made it clear he did not agree with it. Stiffly, the Chief Constable said, 'The team has been introduced to you now, anyway. We can make a start once you've been given all the details we have.'

'I'd like an officer who could be detailed to work with me,' Crow said. 'A detective-sergeant—'

'Detective-Inspector Jones will act,' the Chief Constable said flatly.

Crow almost smiled. These people were pulling no punches. A sergeant, they felt, would have to take too many orders, so give Crow an inspector, a man with some initiative and we can ensure that we remain in control of the situation. The senior officers can go about their business, Crow can supervise and co-ordinate and overlook and advise but he won't be able to control.

* * *

Detective-Inspector Jones. A big man, tall as Crow but running to bulk where Crow remained lean and bony. They'd make a fine pair, physically. He saw the same thought in Jones's eyes and immediately decided he could do worse than work with this man. Jones at least had the capacity to observe himself as well as others and had a sense of humour for all that his brown eyes were as sad as a spaniel's.

'Perhaps you could put me in the picture?' Crow said to Dewi Jones.

The knuckles of Jones's right hand were knobbly with old breaks. He sucked at them thoughtfully as with his left hand he extracted the folder from the filing cabinet and handed it to Crow.

'That's about all we've got so far. The Chief Superintendent has already organised a massive enquiry, door to door, throughout the area and he'll feed in any results once they've been sifted. Chief Inspector Brown is co-ordinating the lab work and as soon as they come up with anything new he'll let us know—'

'I gather it isn't an easy task they have at the lab,' Crow said.

Jones inspected his knuckles and grimaced.

'They haven't. Thing is, the body was down in that shaft for some time. . .the rate of decomposition wasn't high apparently because of the atmosphere or something, but rats had got at the body for sure and there's a few bits missing after the minor falls when they were trying to get the body out. Nothing vital, like, but it's meant some initial difficulties for the pathologists.' He shook his head. 'It certainly gave Dai Chippo a bad turn. Anyway, all the details of what we've got are in there, sir.'

Crow sat down in the chair beside the window. It had stopped raining and the evening streets were shining damply. He pushed the file across the table.

'I'll take that with me to my hotel. I can go through the details later. I'd rather have you tell me about it first.' When Jones looked surprised, Crow added, 'You'll be able to give me facts, but you'll also give me impressions the file won't contain. I can learn things more quickly from your account than from the file.' And, he failed to add, I can learn more about you, Inspector Jones, and that's no bad thing, if we're to work together.

Jones perched himself on the edge of the desk and placed one broad hand on the file. He frowned at it for a moment, marshalling his thoughts.

'Well, what we have so far is this. The body is that of a woman of about thirty years of age. She was well dressed, not too flashy or expensive, but well dressed. She knew what she was about. A few items of a personal nature were missing – handbag, purse, keys and so on, but in the main her clothing, apart from shoes, seems to have been complete. Certainly she had not been subjected to sexual assault, and her underclothes were intact. From the state of her legs and coat we are assuming she was dragged along towards the shaft — there were some splinters of wood in her thigh and the lab boys have a few other items, dirt, rust and so on — but we can't be positive about all this because she could have picked all these things up down there on the rubble.'

'Was she dead before she ended up in the shaft?'

'Dead, or unconscious. The cause of death was probably strangulation, although her neck is also broken — possibly by the fall. When she was pushed through into the shaft — a piece of timber was removed, incidentally, and then replaced after she dropped — she fell straight to the first level, struck the platform there and rolled into the level itself. That's where Dai Chippo found her.'

Crow nodded thoughtfully.

'So you're working on the assumption that the shaft was merely a hiding place for the body, not the method of murder.'

'That's it, sir. And a bloody good place it would have been too, but for that fall at the first level. If she'd have gone straight down we'd never have found her.'

'Nor, presumably, would you have found her if the dog had not been lost.'

Dewi Jones agreed.

'All right,' Crow said. 'The next and obvious question is. . .who was she?'

Jones looked as doubtful as a hesitant virgin, his sad eyes wide and serious.

'A good question, sir. And we've got no answer yet. What we do know is, she wasn't local.'

'On what do you base that assumption?'

'Well, first of all we've been through the missing persons files for the Rhondda and there's no one missing who would be answering the description we got of her: about thirty, brunette, about eight stone, blue eyes, good teeth, married, five foot three in height—no, there's no one we've heard of who fits that description.'

'You said she was married?'

'Wedding ring.'

'Mmm. All right, so there's no one in the files.'

'Another thing,' Jones said, 'is that her clothes aren't local. At least, most of them aren't. Her tights and bra were bought in Cardiff, we're pretty sure of that, even though we can't trace the actual purchase date, of course But her topcoat, a pretty bright affair, brown and white, it was bought in a store called Binns in Middlesbrough.'

'So she might have come from the north-east?'

'Or been there shortly before she died. Anyway, the Chief Super is working on that assumption, and he's started to make enquiries up there.'

'He's been busy,' Crow said drily.

Jones allowed a slight smile to touch his lips. 'We got to show we're as efficient as the Murder Squad, sir.'

'You seem to need little advice. I begin to wonder why I'm here.'

Jones hesitated, then grinned. 'You're having me on, sir. You know as well as I do that all this is preliminary stuff. We have a long way to go even when we know who she is. This all happened months ago, trails are cold as ice and chances are we'll never find out who it was done her in. At least, we know we won't work it out — but you might.'

'You mean you might, if the Murder Squad *advises* you.'

Crow was sorry he said it, as soon as the words were out. He tried to remove the bite of discontent from the words, surrounding them with a smile, but Jones was not easily fooled. Nor was he one to close up, as those others would have done.

'It'll work out, sir.'

'I'm sure,' Crow said briskly. 'Still, you say the body was in the shaft for some time.'

'We think she went in on the sixth of June, sir.'

Crow raised his heavy eyebrows. 'As precise as that?'

'There was the return stub of a train ticket in the pocket of her coat. It was bought on the sixth of June — we've checked it out. She came up from Cardiff on that day. She never went back.'

'Day return ticket?'

'That's it, sir.'

Crow folded his arms and leaned back in his chair. 'So this woman, who might have come from the Middlesbrough area, turns up in Cardiff, buys a day return ticket to—'

'Ystrad Rhondda.'

'Gets off the train, and never goes back. Instead, she ends up down a mine shaft. All right, what questions do we need to find answers to, Inspector?'

Jones grinned. 'You want my *advice*, sir?'

'Only to see if it accords with mine, of course.'

Jones laughed, and his sad eyes were crinkled at the corners with pleasure. 'Well, as I see it, sir, we have several questions that need answering. First, who was she? Second, why did she come to the Rhondda? Third, who did she meet here? Once we have those answers, we can really start work.'

'There is one question you missed,' Crow said.

'Sir ?'

'How long she stayed in the valley before she died.' Crow rose, walked to the window, peered out at the damp streets. His reflection seemed to peer back at him, the bald dome of a head, deep-shadowed eyes, a death's head mirrored against a dark rainy background.

'She had a day ticket, and maybe she didn't return because she was dead. There could have been other reasons for not returning. We don't know she died on the sixth. So we need to find out how long she stayed in the valley.'

He turned his head, looked at Jones.

'Alive.'

* * *

He had Tuesday afternoon and evening clear, and everyone knew the pattern — it was worked out with the other fish-fryers in the valley on a rota basis, even though the thought of anyone's trade being more than purely local was laughable. It gave them a feeling of togetherness, in any case; even a feeling of offering a service of a professional nature, like doctors and dentists, if they worked on a rota. And it suited Dai to have Tuesday afternoon off. It was a good day, in more ways than one. Other shops closed on Wednesdays. And men who might take a Monday off because of a beery weekend, or a Friday off in anticipation of one, would always work on a Tuesday. So it was a good day.

This particular Tuesday was a bright sunny day, and there was a promise of a late heat wave, but Dai was somewhat morose. To start with, Margaret had played hell with him last night because he hadn't left his underclothes where they should have been left for the wash. Unlike every other woman in the valley she washed on Tuesday mornings, not Mondays. There's perverse. And then she had decided not to go down to Pontypridd for her usual shopping expedition. The mountain wasn't the same without Gyp, so it had to be the Club – and Charlie Dick, his usual snooker opponent, was in bed with a broken leg. Playing football for the Wednesday League last week. So Dai left the Club early and walked down through Pentre about four in the afternoon, feeling pretty miserable.

It was only to pass the time, before going back into the shop premises and Margaret that he stopped to speak to Martin Evans as he got out of his car.

Dai didn't know Martin Evans very well, which was surprising since Dai knew most of the people in Pentre. But there were a number of reasons for this. To begin with, Martin Evans wasn't a local man. He had come to the valley several years previously and bought out Old Man Enoch who had all but done for the long-established estate agency of Enoch and Morgan, on the hill opposite Dai. It had picked up when Martin Evans took it over, not a great deal, because Evans certainly wasn't a go-ahead businessman. He seemed to keep himself very much to himself, for a Welsh Canadian, or American, or whatever he was. But the fact he wasn't truly local was one reason why Dai didn't know him too well.

A second reason was Martin Evans's reticence. He was not inclined towards small talk, he wasn't a member of any of the Clubs, he lived a bachelor existence in a well-appointed house in Ton and was looked after by a housekeeper called Maureen McCarthy who was sixty-three, fourteen stone and as exciting as a lump of sour dough. If Dai ever had need for a housekeeper, it wouldn't be her kind he'd look for! So Martin Evans was probably queer, Dai had decided long ago.

Indeed, he had also decided that in sheer business terms it was probably Ceinwen Williams who kept the estate agency on its feet. Martin Evans made few business contacts but Ceinwen was well enough known. She was small and slim, rather shy, nervous — too nervous for Dai who liked a bit of life in his women — but good-looking in her own way. If he had been in Martin Evans's shoes Dai would have thought of marriage to Ceinwen — would probably have been forced into it! After all, Ceinwen had come to work for Martin, travelling every day the three miles from Treorchy, soon after he took over the business. Martin in his bachelor house in Ton, Ceinwen living with her grandmother in Treorchy, meeting every day in the office, working there, saying good night at five-thirty and going their separate ways . . . Evans had never even been known to take her home, not even when it was raining. He must be queer.

But for some reason, this particular Tuesday, he was not averse to conversation.

'Hello, Martin,' Dai said.

'Hello', Martin Evans said, and stood with one elbow on the open car door, looking at Dai. 'How's business?'

He had a curious accent. His voice was deep and resonant and he had the flat vowel sounds that one heard throughout the valley, but his North American accent was like a bad imitation of an amateur actor playing in *Death of a Sales*man. Like that production in the Workmen's Hall Theatre. Dai was never sure whether Martin Evans tried to affect a 'transatlantic' accent but failed to hide his Welsh vowel sounds, or had transplanted those vowel sounds on to his real American accent in an attempt to communicate adequately. It wasn't something you could ask a man.

'Business, like always,' Dai said, 'is up and down. And you?'

'Usual.' Evans said in a non-committal tone. 'You . . . you've had a fair number of people buzzing around this last week, though.'

'Huh, it's information they've been after, not chips.'

Martin Evans closed the door of the car. 'About the body in the pit?'

'What else? It's natural, I suppose, but all I want to do is forget about it. Now, don't get me wrong, I don't mind talking about it because, well, you've not been like all the others, you didn't come chasing around and goggling and all that, like. Your reasons for asking will be different – not bloody curiosity. I suppose you'll be wondering yourself if you ever saw her?'

Martin Evans was not an outgoing person; his emotions were not reflected in his face. He had grey eyes that held a distant look; he rarely smiled, though when he did it seemed to transform his serious visage and make him seem charming; and the passivity of his craggy features lent weight to his general air of withdrawal. Yet Dai felt something was happening to Martin Evans; in some way he had been affected by Dai's last words.

'I don't understand,' he said after a moment. 'How do you think I might have seen her?'

Dai shrugged, watching those cool grey eyes with care. 'Oh, I don't know. It's just that the back of your premises, where you got your own office, it looks out on to the hillside doesn't it? And from there you'd get a view of anyone walking up towards the Bwylffa. It just occurred to me you might have wondered whether you'd actually ever seen the dead woman, walking up there, I mean.'

A smile notable for its control appeared on Martin Evans's face. He shook his head. 'I wouldn't even know whether it was the same woman, would I, even if I'd seen any woman up there. The police have issued no description. In fact, they've been pretty close about the whole thing.'

'That's because they haven't got much to work on. But they have issued a general description — and described what she was wearing. Didn't they come around to ask you if you'd seen her?'

Martin Evans shrugged, looked casually around him as though seeking some way of avoiding the question. 'They came and they asked. But I told them I don't spend my time in the office staring out of the back window. And I go home to Ton in the evenings. So I saw no woman walking up towards the Bwylffa.'

'Nor in the street? In her brown and white coat?'

Evans's grey eyes held a hint of calculation as they stared at Dai Chippo. 'You seem well informed on her dress.'

'I found her down the Pit, remember?'

Evans considered carefully before replying. 'This woman . . . when was it she was supposed to be around here in Pentre?'

'June.'

Coldly, Evans said, 'I can't even remember if I saw you in the street in June, let alone a . . . stranger.'

The pause was an odd one. It was as though Martin Evans had considered the word, almost rejected it in seeking a better one, but had been forced to employ it. And had employed it unwillingly.'

'Aye,' Dai said thoughtfully, with a frown on his face. 'I don't think they've found out just who the woman was, yet. Let alone what she was doing around here. Stranger, indeed.'

Martin Evans squinted up into the sunshine. There were no clouds massed above the hills, it was a perfect afternoon, and the Bwlch-y-Clawdd was sharply etched against the blue sky, its lower slopes darkened by the Forestry Commission plantations, its round-shouldered bulk heavy and somnolent in the sunshine.

'In for a heat wave, I believe,' Evans said.

'Could be.'

'Yes . . . well . . .'

It was the stumbling end to a difficult, stilted conversation but Martin Evans seemed unwilling to break away. He hesitated, looking about him at hills and sky, with a set expression on his face. Confused, Dai waited, was on the point of taking his leave when Martin Evans suddenly took courage and asked the question in his mind.

'Did . . . did you ever see her, Dai? Before you went down the shaft, I mean?'

Dai Chippo had a swift image, a brooch flashing in his mind's eyes, bright and sinful. He felt cold. 'No,' he said. 'Never did.'

* * *

The office premises of Morgan and Enoch, Estate Agents, consisted of a terrace house in which a wide window had been fitted years ago. This was the main unit of conversion; inside, there was a short passageway leading to two rooms—first on the right, the reception area, second on the right Martin Evans's office, looking out to the hillside at the back. There had been a flat at the top of the stain but it had not been used since Evans had bought the firm and the premises.

Ceinwen Williams sat in the reception-room. Her desk was formica-topped and bore a typewriter and a telephone. A large table fronting her desk was covered with loose sheets advertising properties for sale, and on the wall were two prints and a large map of the Rhondda with a number of small flags pinned to it, like an operations map in a military campaign. It was Ceinwen's idea and introduced an element of aggressive salesmanship that was essentially foreign to her nature. She was small, quiet, reserved but efficient. She was a sensitive soul, the neighbours said. Martin looked through the open doorway and smiled at her. She smiled back.

'Cup of tea?'

'Please.'

He walked along the passageway to his own office and then crossed the room, stood by the window, staring up at the hill. He could see the shoulder of the mountain where it swung across, sedge-green, to the first rise of the old slag heaps, black scars on the face of the mountain but greening over as years went by. The straight, uncompromising roadway ran directly up to those tips, and the level of the old Bwylffa pit. He could just see the top of the wheelhouse, stark and black against the blue sky. He had seen the lights up there last week as he had stood here in the office and watched them work to recover the thing that was in the shaft. . .

'Here you are, Martin,' Ceinwen said.

He swung around, surprised. 'That was quick.'

'The kettle was already boiling in the back room. I thought you'd get back by this time . . . Did you persuade him to buy the house in Gelli?'

'You know I could never persuade a client to do anything. You'd already sold it to him.'

Ceinwen smiled. It brought a light to her blue eyes and softened the lines of her face so that she seemed to shed ten of her thirty years. 'We just work well together . . . a good partnership,' she said.

'Yes.'

She looked at him and the smile faded. She sat down, handed a cup of tea across to him as he took the chair behind his desk, and then watched him as he sipped at it. They sat in silence for a while, looking at each other, unsmiling.

'I think we'll get a buyer for the house in Maindy Road,' she said.

'Good.'

He stared at his tea. Ceinwen waited for a little while and then she said, 'What's the matter, Martin?'

He looked at her quizzically. 'Nothing. What should be the matter?'

'Don't play with me. I've known you long enough, and well enough, to be aware of the fact you're disturbed. Something is troubling you.'

'Nothing.'

Silence fell again. His eyes strayed to the window. 'What will you be doing this evening, Ceinwen?'

She sat very quietly in her chair, looking at her hands. 'What I do most nights. I'm knitting that cardigan for little Jimmy down the road. I think there's a play on the television later.'

'Yes. I shall watch it. You . . . you miss your grandmother, don't you?'

Ceinwen put her head on one side, like a shy bird, and smiled. Softly, she said, 'There are many people I miss. My mother. . . my father, even. But yes, I miss Gran Parry, perhaps most of all. She was important to me when I was growing up because she was home. Later, when I came back to look after her, I was repaying her for bringing me up but I think, you know, I was coming home to feel at home again, safe, and protected. And she was able to help. But you know that too, Martin. Yes, I miss her, I miss her dreadfully. There are times when I wake in the house and think she's still there. The feeling can be so real, Martin, I can almost feel her presence. You know what I mean?'

Martin's eyes were fixed on hers.

'I know exactly what you mean. In the dark hours, the dreaming hours, the important realities come into their own. It's when what's past comes alive again, if you want it.'

Ceinwen's cup rattled against her saucer and the sound seemed to startle Martin; he looked away from her and glanced towards the window again. He frowned. 'There are other things people want to forget, and can't.'

'Martin, you are worried about something.'

'No, Ceinwen, really I'm not.' He smiled at her, leaned forward to pat her hand almost protectively. 'I think I'm just tired, that's all. And this business up above us, on the hill, the shaft . . . I don't know, it's unsettled me somehow.'

'I wondered whether it was that,' Ceinwen said. 'The way you've been staring up towards the Bwylffa.'

'I'm just tired,' he said quickly. He sipped his tea. 'Did I hear that Sammy Feeney died last week?'

'Yes. He was ninety, you know. There's a funny thing, though . . .'

'What?'

'Lily Jenkins.'

Martin Evans frowned. He had met Mrs Jenkins, but it had been some time ago, and he couldn't remember . . . Then it came back to him. Most streets in the Rhondda had a Lily Jenkins. They were of an old breed and they were always elderly — even when they were young. Lily

Jenkins herself was probably well over seventy now but she would have looked much the same when she was thirty as she did now, Martin guessed. A big woman, square-built, a face constructed on severe lines, experience of hunger and death and strikes and pit disasters and unemployment scoring her mouth and her cheeks until she resembled a raddled apple, rough skin, dry, dying.

And Death was her trade.

She was no professional; she worked from no Chapel of Rest or Undertaker's Funeral Parlour, She always came before the undertaker, to sit in the death watch while life slipped away from her friend or acquaintance. She took upon herself the physical burden of relatives' grief, she gave them respite from sick-bed and deathbed. And when the time came she laid them out, nightshirt replacing long pants, nightdress replacing coarse woollen with cotton. When the undertaker finally arrived the deceased was ready, eyes closed, arms crossed, peaceful. It was Lily Jenkins's way; it was the valley's way. Or had been. The ones who lived like Lily Jenkins were old now, and the old ways were dying. Young people had different ideas. They didn't even dress like Lily did, and had done all her life, severely, in dark clothes. Mourning clothes.

'I remember her,' he said. 'Black dress. Lives next street up from you.'

'Yes. Thing is, she didn't come down to Sammy Feeney.'

'No?'

Ceinwen detected the lack of understanding in his voice and flickered a little smile towards him. 'You won't see it as I do. Thing is, Lily is like an institution. For as long as I can remember she's been around the street, always the same. She never married, and somehow she's always been there to comfort people, you know? To be at their side when they're dying, and to lay them out when they're dead. The old folk like things done that way — expect it. But she didn't come down to Sammy.'

'I don't follow. . .'

Ceinwen shook her head.

'Well, Sammy Feeney was her generation — older, I know, but of the same outlook, you know? He's been ill for months but she didn't go near. And now he's dead, and she hasn't gone to see to him. I know Sammy's daughter — and she's sixty — was very upset about it. But Lily Jenkins hasn't been out of the house really, not for months. I don't know that someone shouldn't get the doctor to her. I mean, she sits there by herself, and surely, if she doesn't do the laying out what's left in life for her? Cooking mince pies for the neighbours at Christmas, and that's about it. I've been wondering whether we shouldn't have a word with Father Power about it — Sammy was Catholic, but he'd still have expected Lily, you know, though most of her friends are chapel. . .'

Martin Evans allowed his attention to wander. The conversation, and Ceinwen herself, were becoming typical Rhondda in outlook, scope, and limitation. They were concerned with the basic truths in the community: social chatter, religion, death, socialism. Rugby was left to male conversations. The rest. . .

It was like the sky outside that window. Endless, purposeless, drifting forever in a void; the words came and went and the people came and went and they were all the same, there was no escaping the essential sameness and the futility of it all. Ceinwen had been different for a while but she was changing, settling into the pattern and the rut that was life in the valley. Perhaps he was too.

He looked at her. Thirty. Just a few lines around her soft eyes; sad lines. A face that could brighten in excitement in its way. Pleasant, quiet, soft. Many people had said she would make someone a good wife. A few had said to Martin Evans that he ought to marry her.

A spinster in Treorchy; a bachelor in Ton. Only three miles, but a world apart.

He put down his cup abruptly. It rattled with an unexpected violence in the saucer and Ceinwen looked up, surprised. She stopped speaking when she saw the strain in Martin Evans's craggy features.

'Stop it, Ceinwen,' he said abruptly. 'Stop it. There's been talk enough of death.'

* * *

Ceinwen left for home at four-thirty. After she had gone Martin Evans unlocked his desk drawer and took out the letter, dropping the envelope back into the drawer. He sat staring at the letter for a long time. At last he locked the drawer once more, walked to the window, lit the edge of the letter with his cigarette lighter and watched the paper curl and flame. He dropped the last corner out of the window. The ash drifted in the barely existent breeze and was dissipated on the hill.

Martin Evans went home.

* * *

The late heat wave that Dai Chippo and Martin Evans had discussed turned into reality. The valley sweltered under a hot sun and the members of the CID and the local police working in Treherbert took off their jackets as they patiently conducted the house-to-house enquiry. The Red Lion was a popular pub and had a well-respected darts team. Its membership was scattered up the valley and other pub teams visited the Red Lion regularly. All the clientele were asked the same questions: only a few stated they had been at the Red Lion on 6th June, all denied ever having seen a woman in a brown and white coat, and the photograph meant nothing to them.

Similar checks were carried out and enquiries made in the houses leading down towards the square and Ystrad station. Regular commuters to Cardiff from Ystrad, Llwynypia, Tonypandy and lower down the valley were questioned, but none was able to say he remembered a stranger on the train on 6th June. Local shop and café owners were quizzed but in each case the police drew a blank. The pile of statements grew as the days advanced, tempers became short, and Dewi Jones suggested they simply were not going to get anywhere.

Crow thought the same until he read through, once more, the reports of interviews conducted with the men who had been present when Dai Chippo had come up out of the shaft with his dog Gyp.

'Tom Bailey,' he said.

Dewi Jones screwed up his eyes, wrinkled his nose, thought for a moment. 'Mine surveyor,' he said at last.

'NCB. He was up at the pithead when Dai came up.'

'Davies spoke to him.'

'That's right.'

John Crow passed the typewritten statement across without saying more and walked across to the window to look out towards the hills above Tonypandy. One thing, the valley looked better in the sunshine. It was even possible to imagine what it must have been like before it was raped by coalmines and terraced houses.

The pits were all gone now, but the narrow streets remained, climbing up the hillsides in regimented lines just below the menacing curves of the slag heaps.

'How did we miss this?' Dewi Jones asked in surprise.

'Fact is, we did,' Crow said shortly, and ran a hand over his bald, domed skull. His palm came away damp. 'We'd better get Davies in again.'

* * *

Dai Chippo had been nervous enough when he had been questioned by Dewi Jones but his nervousness was greater when he saw Chief Inspector Crow seated across the room. It was partly due to Crow's appearance, no doubt: the tall form on which the dark suit seemed to hang, the bony wrists, the lugubrious face below the bald head. But his presence also was disconcerting; there was something menacing about having a senior detective in the room while Dewi Jones asked the same old questions over again.

'You've got a good memory, Dai,' Jones said at last.

'What do you mean by that?'

'Word perfect, you are,' Jones smiled, glanced across to John Crow. 'You'd think he'd memorized it, word for word, wouldn't you?'

'Perhaps he's just telling the truth,' Crow said, with a gentle grimace.

Dai Chippo squirmed and tried to become angry, but temper was damped by nervousness. 'Truth it is, and if the same words come out it's not because I'm a bloody parrot, it's because there's no other way to tell it accurately. And as for my memory—'

'It *is* good,' Dewi Jones interrupted. 'Bound to be. Word for word, this is . . .'

'All right.' Dai Chippo shrugged. 'As you like. But I don't see what you're—'

Dewi Jones put a great ham fist on the table between himself and Dai Chippo. The movement interrupted the fish fryer, who stared at the fist as though it were a threat. Dewi Jones stared at it too, with serious eyes.

'Let me put it to you like this, Dai. You remember all this, you've told it several times, same words. But there's just one thing about it all that isn't right.'

'It's all exactly—'

'Exactly the same as you've said before. But you see, it's not complete.'

Dai Chippo sat very still. His stocky shoulders were squared and his head was up. Carefully, he linked the fingers of his left hand with those of his right. He looked at Crow, considering, then turned back to Dewi Jones.

'It's complete.'

Jones sighed, tapped his massive knuckles on the table like a teacher saddened by a recalcitrant pupil. 'Not according to what other people say.'

‘What other people?’ Dai Chippo asked with a snap in his voice. ‘Bloody gossipers, I suppose, people who go about with nothing else to do than say if I found that bloody woman down in the shaft I must have known she was down there all the time. You don’t want to listen to people like that, Dewi Jones, not if you—’

The horny knuckles rapped this time, peremptory in a demand for silence. The fist bunched, determinedly menacing now. ‘I want to know what happened at the top of the shaft, Dai, when you brought up the dog. I want to know what you said, who you spoke to.’

Silence fell. Dai Chippo looked vaguely puzzled, a frown of indecision on his face. He unlinked his fingers as though they would unpick his memory and he cleared his throat noisily. ‘Well, all right. Easily said. I found the dog, up I came. They helped me out of the bucket and somebody said something like congratulations. After that, Tom Bailey . . .’

‘Aye, that’s right. Yes, tell me about Tom Bailey.’

The frown deepened on Dai Chippo’s face and his eyes became careful, flicking quick glances towards Crow and back again to Jones.

‘He stroked the dog, like, bit nervous he was but he stroked him. Said Gyp looked pretty fit after being a week underground. It was then that I told him about the body of the woman down the pit. I got pretty sick then, at the thought of how Gyp had managed to survive, and what I remembered I’d seen down there.’

John Crow leaned forward. He spoke for the first time. His voice was soft, deceptively gentle. He injected sympathy into Dai Chippo’s nervous veins. ‘I appreciate it must have been quite a shock for you, Mr Davies. Perhaps that’s why, in the aftermath of that shock, you might have done something, said something you probably forgot later.’

Dai Chippo did not want Crow’s sympathy; it frightened him. He squirmed away from it, shook his head doggedly.

'I don't know what you're talking about. I can remember everything I did or said. I don't know what you're after . . .'

Crow stood up, paced across the room with his long stride and stood over the shopkeeper. Dai looked up, and began to rise.

'Stay where you are, Mr Davies. You may well be right in what you say — you remember everything. Perhaps it's Mr Bailey who's wrong. But what we can't understand is why he should have reported your conversation with him the way he did. He would have no reason to use the words he used, if they were not true.'

'Words, what words?'

'Perhaps Inspector Jones will read them to you,' Crow said quietly.

Dewi Jones reached for the file on the desk, opened it, selected the sheet of paper and read aloud from it in a flat, emotionless monotone.

'Mr Davies got out of the bucket and I went across to him. He told me Gyp hadn't starved down there in the shaft. He started to walk away and I went with him. His teeth were chattering. I think he was shaken by what he'd seen down there in the pit. Then he showed me the ring, said he'd recognized it in the flash of his headlamp and it was then he'd looked beyond and seen the woman's body. He showed me the ring. It was a sort of round thing — a brooch, I mean, not a ring — with a lightning bolt going through the middle. . .'

'Thank you, Inspector.' Crow stood looking down at Dai Chippo. 'Perhaps you can explain, Mr Davies.'

'Explain? Explain what?' A flush came across Dai Chippo's face, a slow stain of belligerence. 'I don't know what the hell you're getting at.'

'I think you do, Mr Davies.' Crow's voice had taken on a cold edge. 'The brooch. . .'

'All right, I found the brooch, picked it up. . .'

'No. You told Tom Bailey you *recognized* it, not just found it.'

Dai Chippo's mouth opened to protest, to deny, then slowly it closed again. His lips seemed to thin, harden, and his eyes narrowed also so that he was almost squinting up at John Crow. He looked for a moment towards Dewi Jones as though seeking aid, and then in tones marked with dislike he said, 'You got things wrong, Chief Inspector Crow. You're not Welsh, you don't know about these things. Tom Bailey is from Tynybedw Street in Treorchy. Welsh-speaking family; it's his first language. He went to the Welsh school up there.'

'So? His command of English seems adequate enough from this report.'

'Oh aye, his English is good, no doubt about that, but what you got to remember is that sometimes a word sort of slips. You might ask a Welshman how he's doing and he'll say "Very well"; next time you ask he'll say "Very Good". It's hanging on to the right word for idiom, you know what I mean? I said *found,* but when Tom Bailey reported it to you he said *recognized.* All right — just a mistake, that's all.'

'Your mistake, Dai.'

Dewi Jones shifted his bulk and leaned forward, scowling. 'That sort of tale won't wash. Facts: you were shaken seeing that body down there; you said to Tom Bailey you recognized that brooch; each time you've had a chat with us you've been worried to death. Better come clean, Dai. It's no good trying to hold out — you'll just make things difficult for yourself.'

Dai Chippo sat still and no one spoke. Outside, the muted sounds of traffic in the main street through Tonypandy was like the buzzing of bees on a summer afternoon. The three men were silent, Crow and Jones waiting for Dai Chippo to speak, the fish-fryer himself gnawed by doubt and anxiety. It was almost a minute later that he stirred himself, brushed a hand across his face as though removing cobwebs of indecision.

'The hell with it,' he muttered.

'You *did* recognize that brooch?' Crow asked quickly.

Dai Chippo nodded miserably.

'So you knew the woman?'

'No. Never did. Just saw her the once, up on Pentre hill. She was standing there, just below the shop. I saw her, I got an eye for a woman, she was a bit of all right. I walked past her, saw her coat, and she turned and the lamplight gleamed on that brooch. I remembered it, when it flashed like that, just the same way, down in the shaft. But I never knew her, just saw the brooch.'

'You saw it just the once, and *remembered* it?'

Crow's tone was incredulous and Dai Chippo looked miserable, but defiant. He nodded his head.

'That was the way of it.'

'All right. When did you see her? What time was it?'

'About ten in the evening. Getting dark. They'd turned on the lights . . . maybe it was ten-thirty, can't be sure.'

'And the date?'

'June the sixth.'

Crow looked at Dewi Jones but the inspector's head was lowered as he made notes on the pad in front of him.

'You don't remember the time,' Crow said slowly, 'but you remember the date with precision.'

'Well, it fits doesn't it? It's the date stamped on the ticket you found in her pocket, isn't it?'

This time Jones's head came up and his glance met Crow's. There was an angry coldness in Crow's eyes and Jones got the message: the valley people might close their mouths when an English policeman passed their way, but the inbred gossiping didn't stop when Welshman spoke to Welshman, whether he was a policeman or not. Jones didn't like it and his mouth was hard. It was a criticism of his men, his force, and Crow's annoyance was justified.

'I'll see who let it out,' he said bitterly.

Crow nodded, turned back to Dai Chippo and asked, 'All right, it fits, but have you any other reason for thinking it was the sixth?'

'Very good reason. The sixth was a Tuesday, right? The shop closes on Tuesday afternoons, doesn't open till Wednesday lunchtime. That's why I was out in the street that time of night. Been to the Club. If we'd have been open that night I'd still have been serving, getting ready to close a while after the pubs emptied.'

'Your wife—'

'Mrs Davies,' Dewi Jones interrupted sourly, 'wouldn't let Dai out at night, except Tuesdays. You're under her thumb, good and proper, aren't you, Dai? And the gossip about the date. . .that was in the shop, was it? Which wife of which copper told you that titbit, hey?'

'*Diawlch*, man . . .'

'When were you in Middlesbrough last, Mr Davies?' Crow asked, cutting across Jones's embittered tones.

'Middlesbrough?' Surprise raised Dai Chippo's voice, emasculated it. 'Never been there in my life, man!'

'Durham? Newcastle upon Tyne?'

Dai Chippo shook his head. 'Not been up there. Went to Whitby once, when I was in the Army, and stayed a while at Catterick Camp, but I never did get further north than that, ever. Not ever.'

Crow walked back across the room and folded his arms. He lowered his head, thrusting it forward like a bird of prey about to strike.

'So it wasn't up there you met Donna Stark?'

'Donna Stark? Who the hell is . . .' Dai Chippo stopped speaking, his mouth opened and closed and he began to blink rapidly. He swallowed hard.

'The woman in the pit . . . you know who she is?'

'The woman in the pit, the woman whose brooch you recognized, the woman you saw at the top of Pentre hill on the 6th of June, yes, we know who she is. We received the information today, it'll be in the newspapers in the morning. Durham police finally traced her. Mrs Donna Stark. And you still say you didn't know who she was?'

* * *

After Dai Chippo had left the room Crow stared moodily at Dewi Jones. The inspector was still frowning, still thinking about leaks of information, but conscious of the silence he looked up to Crow.

'Well, sir?' He grimaced. 'What do you think?'

'He's lying.'

'Could be he did just meet her on the hill . . .'

'No,' Crow said decisively. 'He's lying, of that I'm certain. It doesn't ring true — he would never have recognized a brooch on a woman after months like that, not when he had seen her only once. That man hasn't told us everything, not yet.'

'We could hold him, sir, question—'

Crow shook his head. 'We'll let him stew a bit, wait until he starts to relax and think the worst is over, then come after him again. I'm going up to the north, to learn a bit more about the deceased Mrs Stark. After that, maybe we'll have something to throw at our fish-frying friend, something that'll make him say a few more words than he's inclined to do at the present.'

'The Chief Super is still up there, sir,' Jones said doubtfully.

Crow looked at Jones and smiled; the smile became conspiratorial, and after a moment Jones joined in it.

'And with a bit of luck, maybe I'll manage to avoid him,' Chief Inspector Crow remarked.

CHAPTER 3

John Crow enjoyed the drive north.

To begin with there was the drive itself. Once the car had left the Heads of the Valleys Road and swept past the industrial areas, there were the dipping curves of Monmouthshire to be enjoyed. The road became uninteresting as it sliced monotonously through Birmingham and Staffordshire, with only the distant lift of Cannock Chase to suggest hills and trees, but once past Cheshire there was the promise of the most scenic motorway in England. The traffic was moderately heavy, with people still streaming like lemmings for the Lake District, but the hills rose magnificently beyond, the Pennines loomed up, the road drove its way through rugged cliff faces and they crossed Shap and began the run down to Carlisle.

They had made one stop shortly after they passed Stafford; they made a second, before they left the motorway outside Carlisle and took the Newcastle road, cutting off across the Military Road to avoid the heavier traffic and to afford Crow a few glimpses of the Wall at

Housesteads. After that it was a swift, undulating drive towards Newcastle.

And this afforded Crow's second enjoyment: the thought of meeting Frank Luffman again. It had been at least ten years since they had last met; they had known each other for a long time before that, professionally and socially (Martha still wrote to Joyce Luffman from time to time); and since Frank had given up his diving activities and was now acting merely as an office-bound head of the skin team assisting in river searches, it was going to be easier to spend some time with him and learn a few local facts without going through official channels and perhaps upsetting the Chief Superintendent already working in the area.

But first of all, Crow had to inform the Chief Superintendent that he was in Newcastle, and obtain any details already gathered concerning Donna Stark. The Chief Superintendent offered no objections — he was about to return to Cardiff anyway, having completed his investigations in Newcastle and Durham, and was quite prepared to hand over the file to Crow.

John Crow studied it that evening, while he had a drink in the quiet hotel he had picked out for himself in Jesmond. He sat in the lounge bar quite late that evening, reading the reports and staring at the photographs of Donna Stark.

There were three of them. Two were merely snapshots and did little more than emphasise that she had a good figure and dressed smartly. The third was a professional job, taken in a Durham studio perhaps five years earlier.

Crow stared at it for a long time.

A murder investigation usually held a basic problem for the investigator — he never really knew the dead person, never really learned what he or she had been like. Everything was second-hand — impressions, statements, letters, diary entries, the ephemeral particles that were all that remained of a person, flickers from a candle that had gone out, shadows on a wall. Crow felt this deeply; he was a sensitive man unable to treat a cadaver merely as just another corpse to deal with in professional terms. It had been a person and he felt unable to adequately cope with his job unless he knew what that person had *been.*

Photographs helped.

They helped not only in what they showed as in what they hid. This photograph from the Durham studio showed head and shoulders of a blonde woman, hair parted straight, almost severely, but falling more casually across one eye. Her face was square, slightly heavy-jawed, but she had been a handsome woman with a resolute mouth and bold aggressive eyes. Those eyes interested John. The woman who had stared so aggressively at the camera had also taken the precaution to hide those eyes. The make-up was heavy—perhaps she had had fair, almost invisible brows and lashes and needed the security of pencil and eye-shadow. But her lashes were not her own: heavy and black they were like a protective curtain — she could lower them and escape, conceal and run. But the camera had held no fears for her.

As he sipped his lager Crow grimaced, thought himself fanciful. But the fact remained, Donna Stark had had something to fear in the end. Maybe she had feared it even then. Aggression and confidence — take the world, shake it, milk it, use it; caution and precaution—keep escape routes available, watch for danger, plan, run, escape . . .

* * *

It was interesting.

James Klein also was interesting, but in a different way. John Crow went to see him next morning, driving across the Tyne Bridge, along the motorway to Durham, through the town and up among the quiet closes near the University. Klein lived in a mock Tudor cottage that would have cost him a considerable amount of money with its long green lawns, view of the Cathedral and the river and the distant Cleveland hills. But it hadn't cost him what Crow had guessed, for the file said he rented the property.

The file also allowed Crow to guess why Klein would be, essentially, a man who needed a front for his own inadequacies. They were not apparent in his bearing or his appearance. He was of middle height and stockily built, well dressed in a lemon shirt open at the throat and grey, well-cut slacks. He held his shoulders well back, hands locked behind his trim waist, and his thick, slightly greying hair was as carefully placed as the expression on his face. He oozed the confidence and control of a man whose career was built on quicksand; he showed the smooth social ease of a man who had had to claw up to his present position in the social community. His voice was resonant and deep, his accent modulated, the offending Tyneside smoothed away.

'Chief Inspector Crow, I'm pleased to meet you.'

He made it sound as though he meant it, but his cold eyes had seen too many policemen to like seeing another.

'I'm rather surprised, I admit, to receive another visit — it's as though it's open hunting season around here for CID men at the moment, but of course I've no objection to helping in any way I can. Not that there's much I can do to help, as I told the Chief Superintendent only last —'

Crow nodded, turned, looked at the settee and Klein made a hasty gesture, offering him the seat. Crow sat down; the leather was smooth and expensive. He looked up; Klein remained standing near the stone fireplace, hands still locked behind his back.

'I would appreciate your co-operation Mr Klein,' Crow said softly. 'I realise you have already made a report to the Chief Superintendent, but it's always useful in matters such as these to have two opinions—'

'Like doctors,' Klein said, and laughed.

'Much the same sort of job in a way,' Crow agreed, and smiled. 'Make an incision, turn aside the protective skin, slice through the concealing fat, get at the truth underneath. Even if it's cancerous.'

Klein did not care for the comparison he had started. Brusquely, he said, 'Yes, well, I gather your visit is in connection with Donna Stark.'

'That's right. I'd like you to tell me about her.'

'I've already told the—'

'Tell me how you came to meet her, how long you were together, when you last saw her, what she was like. Anything. Everything. You know what I mean?'

Klein knew. He was no fool. Crow didn't want the obvious answers, the times and dates and places that the Chief Superintendent had asked for. He wanted facts, but he wanted impressions too, and reasons. Klein knew. He didn't want to.

'There's not a lot I can tell you I haven't told already. I mean, it's all been taken down in the statement I signed—'

'I've seen the statement. It tells me you met Donna Stark at a nightclub some years ago. You knew her for about two years, then you started an affair with her, she lived with you for about thirteen months, then you and she quarrelled, she left, and you've heard nothing from her or about her since. Right?'

Klein nodded stiffly.

'Now tell me the rest,' Crow said softly.

Klein studied him for a moment, let his cold eyes flicker over the long bony figure. He considered.

'You're Murder Squad.'

'That's right.'

'Taking notes?'

'No notes.'

Klein grimaced. His arms relaxed somewhat, he withdrew his hands from behind his back. He walked the room, poured himself a drink from a decanter of whisky on the cabinet in the corner and then walked back, stared out of the window across the lawns to the Cathedral.

'I've got a lot to lose, Chief Inspector.'

Crow made no reply. After a moment, Klein sipped his whisky then turned decisively, as though he had reached a decision. It was a good performance; Crow knew nevertheless that Klein would be saying nothing he did not want to say, giving nothing away he was not prepared to give.

'I'll put it to you straight,' Klein said, gesturing with his glass. 'You'll know all about me if you haven't already found out, so I'll tell you. I was born in the Scotswood Road and I went through the lot . . . juvenile courts, Borstal, two years inside. Then I struck lucky, and saw sense. I got tied up with a man called Brown who gave me an inside run and I've been straight ever since. I learned the car business in my twenties and I threw over my old friends. I had a down when I was thirty-five, and it threw me for a while—but I bounced back, and here I am now. I built up my own car-hire business and it's solid, well pretty solid anyway. And I moved to Durham, I made good connections. Connections that were too important to be broken by Donna Stark.'

Crow crossed his legs at the ankles and contemplated his cuffed shoes.

'Tell me,' he said.

Klein took another drink then sat down, draping one leg over the arm of the chair. He put his head back, stared at the ceiling and chuckled.

'If anyone had told me twenty years ago I could end up marrying a bird who'd be coming into a fortune when she was twenty-five I'd have thrown him into the Tyne for ribbing me. But that's how life's worked, Inspector Crow. And that's why I couldn't afford Donna Stark.'

'You wanted to get married'

'I intend getting married next month. And don't think this investigation into Donna will stop it . . . Grace knew all about Donna. But Donna had to go—'

He stopped suddenly, his eyes flickering alarm in Crow's direction.

'That is, what I mean . . . look, I met Donna a few years back, she was married, I saw her a few times, we had a few giggles together. But I was going through a bad patch and I needed . . . solace. She gave me it. I didn't see her for a while after that, but when I began to build up the car-hire business she came around again. She was always good in bed, I was fancy free, she'd left her husband, so what the hell! We got together. I fixed her a flat in Chester-le-street and we had a good time. It's in the report, the dates and all that. But then Grace happened.'

'And there wasn't room for two of them.'

'Grace is the one who'll come into money?'

Klein took a stiff drink.

'Money is important. And she's not a bad looking woman. But she told me Donna had to go. So Donna went.'

'Quarrel?'

Klein laughed with a real amusement.

'That's an understatement! She played hell! Tore a strip of skin off my cheek, kicked me where it hurts most, but after I told her a few home truths she went packing. Thing is, Chief Inspector, Donna was a funny woman. She was . . . how can I put it? Tough. She could swear with the best of them. She knew what life was about. She'd seen a lot of it in her thirty years. She'd worked as secretary in some crummy firms before she got a job in a lawyer's office, but it all added up to experience. Tough. But that wasn't all. She could make you feel great. She could make you feel she was innocent. She could act like the original bitch and then make you feel she was a pussy cat. She could twist a man around her finger and make him think he was God Almighty. So she was tough and she was an actress but she was also scared as hell. You know what I mean? She had a few years to make good; she had to take what the good years could give her. She believed that she needed her ship to come in while the sailors were still around because when they'd gone there'd be nothing left in life. She had to make good now, and if that wasn't on, it was time to leave.'

Klein laughed again, and shook his head.

'That's the whole scene, Chief Inspector. It's no good thinking I might have knocked her off because she was getting in my way with Grace. It wouldn't have been necessary, ever. Fact was, Donna Stark could be a bitch and scratch my face open but she was also a realist. There was no percentage in keeping the game going; she knew she'd get nothing more from me, so she cut her losses and went.'

'Where?'

'The greener grass.'

'And that was?'

Klein shook his head. His grey eyes seemed colder than ever, disinterested.

'She said she was going to see Jack Scales. But he wouldn't have been the green grass. A lift over the fence, maybe, but the green grass, that would have to be something different . . .'

* * *

'So what do you think, Frank?'

They stood in the shadow of the Tyne Bridge, leaning on the rail at the darkening quayside as the freighter slipped her moorings and headed downstream for Tynemouth and the North Sea. Frank Luffman had welcomed John Crow in his home at Westerhope, allowed him to be fussed over by Joyce, but when evening had come had pulled him out of the house, driven down to the river and here they now stood in the twilight as the traffic rumbled above their heads across the bridge and the lights of the city twinkled above them.

Frank Luffman lit his pipe and puffed at it, inspected it, lit it again.

'Can't tell you anything about Donna Stark you don't know already. Jimmy Klein now, he's a different kettle of fish. Well enough known on Tyneside.'

'I'd appreciate anything you can give me,' Crow said.

'Aye, well, you've got to remember the limitations on anything I say,' Luffman replied, scratching his lean cheek with the stem of his pipe. 'It's only hearsay. I been with the rivermen a long time up here, we've pulled a few things out of the river in my time, and a few of them have been suicides who couldn't face the consequences of their frauds. I've asked around and I've heard Jimmy Klein could have been one of them, if he'd been a different kind of feller.'

'His background is shady?'

'More than that. Your files will have told you he was a tearaway when he was younger. Maybe he still is, hey?'

'Donna Stark is dead,' Crow said quietly.

'Aye. But Wales is a long way from Tyneside. Still, the picture I've got is much the same as you got it from Klein. Seems he picked up with this girl Stark, lived with her a while, then dropped her when this other piece showed up and flourished her fivers.'

'But what were the things he didn't tell me?'

Luffman smiled, linked his arm through Crow's, drew him away from the rail and together they walked up towards the Manors and Dog Leap Steps.

'The first thing he didn't tell you was he *needs* this marriage to Grace Rendell. He needs her money.'

'His business is shaky?'

'Overstretched. He'll be in water deeper and blacker than the Tyne unless she hauls him out — and believe me, the Tyne is pretty deep and pretty black.'

'Anything else?'

'You mean that's not enough of a motive for murder?'

Luffman's breath grew shorter as they began to climb the narrow steps leading up towards the streets above.

'Ah, well, the rest is the interesting story of what happened after he met Donna Stark but before they lived together.'

'He told me they met in a night club.'

Luffman nodded. He stopped, turned, looked back down the steps towards the dark quayside.

'Bloody hell, since I gave up the swimming a few years back my body's not been the same. Out of bloody breath, on Dog Leap! We're getting old, John!'

'We are.'

'Aye, well they met in a night club, hey? Could be. But there's some who say they had a professional contact as well.'

'What sort of professional contact?'

'Top of the steps, for God's sake, and I'll tell you. All right for you . . .bloody long skinny legs and no belly. . . when you swim and dive and give it up . . . bloody pot . . .'

Grey Street proved easier, the incline still steep but not tearing the breath from Frank Luffman's lungs. They strolled past the Theatre Royal and reached Grey's monument. Luffman leaned against it, watched the people and the cars and shook his head.

'Newcastle's changing.'

'James Klein . . .' Crow said patiently.

Luffman laughed.

'You're too bloody persistent, John. Tynesiders don't like to be rushed. My time in the Met, it was all too pushed. We like to promise the moon, and deliver it. . . one of these days. All right, James Klein. Thing is, he was being chased up for fraud about the time he got really friendly with Donna Stark.'

'He told me he had a down period about then.'

'Down it was,' Luffman said grimly. 'Klein was sales manager of a large firm here in Newcastle – Northeast

Credit it was called. Sounded like a finance firm but it wasn't; dealt in cars mostly, motor dealers, vehicles ranging from three hundred to three thousand quid, good fast turnover. He got the job through some connection he'd made as a youngster but he and his friend Brown—dead now—certainly didn't part friends. The fact was it was suspected for a long time that Klein had been responsible for certain irregularities in the firm's accounts.'

'Suspected?'

'Never proved.'

'So what's this got to do with Donna Stark?'

Frank Luffman nodded across towards the Eldon Centre. 'Come and have a beer,' he said.

* * *

The man who joined them in the bar was small, thin and repressed in appearance. His suit was of quality cloth, perhaps worn for the occasion but his shirt and tie were untidy, collar ends curling, tie not straight. His underwear would be a week old, Crow thought to himself.

He was introduced as Donald Rich. He shook hands but released Crow's bony fingers quickly as though he feared retention of his own. He tried to smile but his mouth was nervous and his teeth were bad and he gave up the effort even before it really started. He accepted the beer Luffman bought, took a long swallow but was in no way encouraged or revived. He seemed to wish very badly that he wasn't there.

'This is Mr Crow,' Luffman said. 'The chap I said would like to have a talk.'

'Yes, Mr Luffman.' Donald Rich did not look at Crow. The prefix 'Mr' did not fool him; he knew Luffman and he knew who Crow was. For that matter Crow was already making a guess about Rich too—he'd seen enough of his kind in the past. A snout and an informer: Rich had all the mannerisms of the cheapest. The best were confident and assured; Rich's kind dwelt on the fringes of information, asked a great deal, got little and gave little. Crow glanced at Luffman, surprised that he would bring such a man to John Crow. Luffman smiled.

'Donald used to work with your friend. At Northeast Credit.'

Crow led the way to the table in the corner. They sat down, Luffman to Crow's left, the two facing the nervous Donald Rich isolated across the table.

'I met Mr Klein for the first time this morning,' Crow said. 'He seems to have done well for himself.'

He could not have chosen a better way of loosening Rich's inhibitions and fears. If the man had been reluctant, rage removed the reluctance; if he had been cautious, bitterness wiped away the caution. He said three words, sharply, obscenely, and left Crow in no doubt as to his feelings towards James Klein.

'You don't think he deserves his . . . ah . . . success,' Crow said quietly.

'He got it by stampin' on other people's faces, Mr Crow. But he'll get it himself, in time, if I has my way he'll get it. The coppers got nothing on him, couldn't fix him, turned on me instead, but I been listenin' and lookin' around, and one of these days when I'm ready I'll be taking a file of papers around to the station and they'll pull him in and throw the book at him."

Crow let the vicious, vehement words die away in silence. Puzzled, he glanced at Luffman and then back to Rich.

'You're keeping a dossier on Klein?'

'I hate the bastard! He cost me three years — and my reputation.'

Donald Rich wasn't a police informer. Crow had misjudged him. He caught the gleam in Luffman's eye and realised Luffman had guessed at Crow's misconception and had been amused. But there was no amusement in Donald Rich. He was full of sourness and hate.

'You'd better explain what you mean,' Crow said. 'You were with James Klein in Northeast Credit. Is that where it happened?'

Rich scowled at his beer. He felt he deserved better than beer out of life and Klein had taken it away from him. He would have forgotten the limitations of his own character and capabilities: he had found the scapegoat for his failures in Klein and his whole life-style would now breed on that hate.

'I was the man who got the credit for the whole thing. I was the one the police turned to when the case against Klein fizzled out. I was the one who got hauled up at the Assizes, got fixed with a term of imprisonment of three years. The barrister I got stuck with. . .you know who it was? Some character just two years out of the mental home! He didn't even read the papers I wrote! I put it all down, I explained in detail how it couldn't have been me, I didn't have the know-how, I didn't have the access to the papers, I was never near the blasted office when the papers were rigged, but did he mention this in court? Did he, hell! He hadn't even read the papers! Legal-aid, you can stuff it!'

Rich tried to drown the fires of his resentment in a long draught of beer. It failed; the heat still burned in him and his eyes glared angrily around the room. Crow leaned forward.

'I haven't got the picture yet, Mr Rich.'

Donald Rich finished his beer. He became sullen, the corners of his mouth drooping, and his eyes stared at the puddle of beer stains on the table in front of him.

'No one's wanted to see this particular picture. Why you, now?'

'Because I brought Mr Crow here, Donald,' Frank Luffman said quietly, tapping out his pipe in an ashtray. 'You know me, I've listened. I've done nothing because there's nothing to be done. You've served your term, you've talked to me, I've listened. All right, now you have a bigger chance. You know Mr Crow's an important man.

He's not bringing you help; he's not offering you any. But he wants to listen. And if he hears the right words, and they fit . . . who knows?'

There was an implied promise in the words, even if they were as non-committal as Luffman could make them, and Crow was vaguely uneasy. It was holding out something to Donald Rich that would probably not be possible to obtain. But Luffman had used the words and John Crow had to go along with them.

'I'm listening, Mr Rich.'

Donald Rich hunched forward over his almost empty beer glass. He rubbed a hand over his jaw; the rasping sound suggested he had shaved none too closely and his shirt cuff was frayed.

'I was at Northeast Credit,' he said huskily. 'I was working on the books — accounts clerk, in James Klein's office. That's why they saddled it on me.'

'Saddled what?'

'The frauds.'

Crow sighed. 'Tell me.'

Before Rich could reply, Luffman tapped his pipe bowl loudly on the table.

'The truth, Donald, remember that!'

For a moment Rich seemed to struggle with himself, eyes flickering, considering whether to go on at all. But he had taken too many body blows and he needed to talk.

'All right, I've done my time. I admit it. I was light-fingered. I was in Accounts, there were opportunities. . .you got to remember, Mr Crow, cars were coming in, the turnover was so quick, checks from the auditors were less than efficient. I tell you, any fool could have milked the company. It was there for the taking and plenty of people took. I didn't see why I shouldn't take too. So that's what I did. I pulled out fifty quid here, fifty there. It was easy. Cash transactions on the cheaper cars, work a fiddle with the salesman out front, no duplicates on invoices and type them up later, split the money . . . It was a system, it worked.'

'But you got caught,' Crow said grimly.

Rich shook his head.

'No. We didn't get caught. I reckon we could have gone on for years. But someone else got greedy. Not us, not the little ones milking the cow for a few drops. Somebody else.' He finished his beer with a quick swallow. Without a word Frank Luffman rose, walked across to the bar to get another round. Crow remained silent until he returned, then leaned forward.

'Go on.'

Rich gripped the handle of the beer mug as though for strength. His eyes failed to meet Crow's but his voice was shaky with anger.

'Look, you got to take what I say on trust and that's something they didn't do in court. But you got to take it because I got no reason to lie now, have I, Mr Luffman? I done my time. But these is the facts! The whole business blew over because Northeast Credit was never a sound proposition anyway. Too many in for a quick quid. And the turnover of cars was rapid. Well, you know how the system works. Customer comes in, you flog him the car. He thinks he's dealing with you when you give him credit; in fact you sell the car to a finance company who give the customer the credit and can take back the car if he doesn't pay. Okay, that's how it goes. But there's credit restrictions on all this. The customer had to stump up a cash deposit before he could get the credit. That's where the fiddles came in.'

'No deposits?' Crow asked.

'No deposits, but forged documents to say they were made and then inflated prices on the cars to cover the fraud. Now let me put it to you straight, Mr Crow. I couldn't have been involved in all that. I didn't have access to the papers, though they said I did. They said it was me who forged the hire purchase documents to avoid the credit restrictions and they dumped the whole thing on me. *But they never produced the evidence.'*

Crow frowned. He leaned back in his chair, tapped the edge of his glass with a bony finger.

'If there was no documentary evidence. . .'

'Ahh . . . well, there *was* one piece of paper,' Rich said reluctantly, 'and they hung the rest on that, but all the real robbing wasn't done by me, I swear. And there was a collection of six sheets which could have proved it. HP documents, forged all right, but not by me. Inter-linked transactions and a name on one of the documents.'

'James Klein?'

Rich grimaced and nodded. Crow considered the matter.

'Klein wasn't arraigned?'

'If you mean he wasn't brought to court the answer's no.'

'But if you knew it was he—'

'I didn't,' Rich asserted indignantly, 'and even if I had I wouldn't have shopped him. I was pleading innocence, remember, and it was only later I worked out what had happened to those papers and who got hold of them.'

'So what did happen to those papers?' Crow asked.

'The first link in the chain was a deal James Klein worked with a car-hire firm who were selling three Mercedes, top-class stuff. He bought them for the firm, and then forged the papers later to resell the cars, but the papers never went through the firm. I saw them, even so. Thing is, what happened to them? I tell you. They was took from the office by a firm of solicitors acting for Northeast Credit. And that was that.'

Crow held up a bony hand.

'Now wait a minute. Let's get this clear. A solicitor who takes papers while acting for a person likely to be prosecuted cannot hold those papers back in the event of a prosecution. He will be called upon to disclose all papers relevant to the case; he would have to hand copies to the prosecution.'

'If he's got them!' Rich jeered.

Crow frowned.

'I don't know what you mean. You told me—'

'I said they was collected by the firm. Then . . . they disappeared.'

'Just disappeared?'

'This wasn't mentioned at the trial,' Luffman said. 'The existence of the papers wasn't even commented upon. It accounts for Klein's non-involvement in the prosecution. The little men like Rich got hammered; Klein, he went free though, as bust as Northeast Credit was.'

'The solicitors . . .'

'Still in business. Respectable firm. Used to be in Eldon Square till the planners pulled it down, rot them. Moved top of Blackett Street now. But forget them, as such. Ask me about Mrs Stark again.'

Crow stared at Luffman, thinking of what he had already heard earlier.

'She worked there?'

Frank Luffman laughed.

'Almost got there, John. No, she used to work there as a receptionist till she moved up in the world.'

'You mean she got married?'

'That's so. To one of the partners. She was still married to him when she first met James Klein. And the marriage was still in existence when the papers disappeared.'

Crow was silent. He was beginning to see bits of the jigsaw form a pattern. Klein was in trouble, Donna Stark helped him out. Later, Donna Stark went to live with Klein . . .

'What happened to her husband?' Crow asked sharply.

Luffman shrugged.

'He left the partnership shortly after Donald here was sent down. No longer in practice, it seems.'

'Were they divorced?'

'No record of it as far as I know.'

'And why did Stark leave the partnership?'

Luffman smiled.

'You'll have to ask them that yourself. But I bet you get damn all out of them about it. They'll tell you he left of his own accord and by agreement. You'd hardly expect them to agree he left because his wife — with or without his connivance — pulled some papers out of the private office in order to get Jimmy Klein off the hook, do you? Even solicitors have a sense of self-preservation.'

'Mmm.' Crow frowned. He looked at Donald Rich, saw the bitterness in the man's eyes staining them like a dark shadow, and he wondered.

'Were you ever in the Rhondda, Mr Rich?'

CHAPTER 4

Dewi Jones was waiting at Crow's hotel when he returned from Newcastle. He seemed pleased to accept Crow's offer of dinner together; he was even more pleased when Crow turned the conversation to sport and Jones was able to discuss the relative merits of Cardiff and Llanelli Rugby Clubs, Glamorgan and Gloucestershire Cricket Clubs, and how good fighters were hungry fighters.

'There were a lot of them around in Wales in the old days,' he said enthusiastically, 'but the Welfare State has killed them off. Me, well, I was pretty good but I would never have *lived* in the same ring with the old ones. They *had* to fight, you see. It was the only way to get a steak in your belly in those days. It was the necessity that pushed them and made them good fighters. There are necessities other than hunger, of course, Being black for instance — it creates a drive in a man that makes him want to succeed. *Need* to succeed. So black fighters make good fighters too. And if you're black and hungry . . . Aye, a man will fight hard if the need is in him. Sometimes it's physical, but it can be emotional too.'

The remark brought Crow's mind away from sport, and the conversation he had deliberately encouraged with Jones in an attempt to break away from the case he was dealing with. It pushed him back to Donald Rich. The man had denied ever having been to Wales, but he may well have had a motive for murdering Donna Stark. If he had felt she was really responsible in some way for his becoming the scapegoat in the Northeast Credit case, there might have been a strong enough need in him to pay her back. Perhaps the thoughts were mirrored in his eyes or in his lugubrious expression, for Dewi Jones fell silent as he finished his sweet. When coffee came he looked up and said, 'Was the trip to the North worthwhile, sir?'

Crow grimaced, stirred some cream into his coffee and looked out of the window to the Cardiff streets.

'I was able to look up an old friend, so there was that to its credit. Apart from that, not a great deal. This man Klein—'

'The one Donna Stark had been living with?'

'Yes. He's got a shady background and maybe reason to want to kill her, whatever he says. He threw her over in favour of another woman, and he says Mrs Stark accepted it. But if she didn't, if she was likely to cause trouble, if she was threatening to break up Klein's impending marriage with Grace Rendell, a marriage on which he was relying to save his car-hire business, well, it could have been reason enough to kill her.'

'But why in Wales?'

Crow sipped his coffee, added some more cream. He had long ago learned nothing in his diet would ever put flesh or fat on his bones. He was committed irrevocably to leanness whether he liked it or not. In fact, it bothered him little even if people did smile when they saw him out with Martha, plump as he was skinny.

'Why in Wales, indeed. Klein suggested she was looking for greener grass once she knew she could get no more cash or security from him. Our information is she went to a former lover, Jack Scales. Now then, have you managed to unearth anything on him?'

'Only that he's here in Cardiff.'

Crow eyed Dewi Jones. The heavy face betrayed no emotion, no excitement, and yet the thought must have been in Jones's mind as it was in Crow's. Scales was in Cardiff; Donna Stark had died in the Rhondda.

Was this the connection they were seeking?

They stopped the car, just after it drove under the railway bridge at the head of Bute Street, and Jones and Crow got out. Crow did not know the area and wanted to see it. He had heard enough of Tiger Bay in the past, but he guessed that the reputation would largely have been one it gained between the wars and things would be quieter now. He guessed right, of course. As the two policemen walked along Bute Street there was some evidence of decay and poverty; peeling paint, dirty windows, corner shops crammed with cheap, shoddy goods, dirty gutters and chip-papers swirling in the roadway. But the cars parked along the street were large enough, if not of recent vintage, and the coloured men who lounged at the corners displayed no interest in the strangers. Some children played in the side streets, noisy as any children, scruffier than many, but the whole scene was no more rundown than many Crow had come across, Areas in London were worse, Birmingham had its streets no better; it was reputation and the proximity of the docks that gave Bute Street its continued tawdry glamour.

'They still get trouble in the pubs, Saturday nights,' Jones said almost apologetically, as though wanting to maintain the street's roughly romantic image.

'They do in most pubs,' Crow said shortly'

'Is this the address we're looking for?'

It was a narrow terrace house, not far from the consulates based near the docks themselves. The door was open, the passageway beyond dark, uninviting and smelly.

At the foot of the stairs was a bowl half-full of stale beer. Indistinguishable black objects lay half submerged in it.

'Cockroaches,' Dewi Jones said. 'My grandmother used to drown them like that — they love beer, put a bowl down and out they come in the dark.'

'DDT works better.'

'But not so much fun for the kids. Ever seen a drunken cockroach trying to escape?'

Crow didn't want to. They climbed the stairs, paused at the first landing, hammered on the door. The old woman who answered directed them above; the bulb on the landing did not work and there was only the dim glow from below to light their way.

Jack Scales was not quick to answer the knocking.

When he finally opened the door it was slowly, to peer around it at the visitors. The fact they were strangers and reasonably well dressed seemed to reassure him.

'Whaddya want?'

He had been drinking and was vaguely belligerent. Stale beer and tobacco gusted out on his breath.

'We're police officers,' Crow said and pushed at the door. If Scales had intended resisting he forgot about it and retreated into the bedsitting-room. It was a mess. The curtains were drawn and their dinginess seemed to emphasise the squalor of the room itself. The bed in the corner was unmade, there were dirty plates and cups on the table, a pile of discarded rumpled clothing lay heaped on the easy chair and the pans on the gas cooker were thick with grease, the accumulation of weeks. Crow wrinkled his nose in distaste.

'Mr Scales?'

'That's right.'

He fitted the room, and yet on the other hand he did not. Scales was about five feet eleven in height, lean but well-muscled in shoulder and arms, and his waist was slim. He looked fit and strong and his face was a handsome one, a proud jutting nose and a broad mouth giving him an air of arrogance. But he was slumped as he stood facing Crow, his mouth was turned down and disappointed, his muscles slack. There was a puffiness about his eye that suggested the drinking was not occasional and the hard muscles of his belly would soon slacken and spread. He was a strong, handsome man going to seed; properly dressed and sober he would make a striking figure, but in shirt sleeves and stained slacks and slippers he looked like a man sliding fast into middle age before his time.

'We want to ask you a few questions.'

'What about?'

'Donna Stark.'

'Bloody hell.'

Scales stood still for a moment, his dark eyes glaring first at Crow and then at Jones. At last he turned away, hauled off his shirt, drew aside the curtain that hid the washbasin in the corner and he proceeded to wash himself, hands, face, neck, shoulders, armpits, with much puffing and grunting as the coldness of the water bit at his heated body. The two policemen watched him. He searched for a towel, found none, so dried himself on the curtain. He would be cleaner by a little, but more sober by a great deal. It had been the object of the exercise. He turned, stood looking at them and slowly pulled his shirt back on. He said nothing.

'When did you last see Donna Stark?' Dewi Jones asked.

Scales grimaced.

'It's no good me saying I don't know who you're talkin' about?'

'None. We've information from the north-east"

'Areet, then. Months ago.'

'How many months?' Crow asked sharply.

Scales tucked his shirt into his trousers with exaggerated care. He looked down, pulled up the zip.

'April, May . . . about then.'

'She died in June.'

Scales continued to stare down at his trousers. He turned slowly, reached for the easy chair, pulled the clothes to the floor and sat down. He let out his breath slowly. When he looked up his eyes shone with a cold light.

'Aye . . . I read about it.'

'When?'

'This week. I just got off the freighter, *Isle of Arran.* Saw it in the South Wales Echo. First I knew. Bit of a shock.'

Dewi Jones grunted. 'That's why you've been soaking the beer?'

Scales turned his pale eyes in Jones's direction; his glance was indifferent.

'I been at the beer because I just got back from sea, because it was a hell of a trip, because I'll never sail with that bloody skipper again, because I got some money to burn, because I've had a couple of women and I need to wash them out of my system . . . and because I like a bloody good skinful.'

Sarcastically, Jones said, 'I thought you might have been drinking to wipe out her memory.'

'I thought you might have been drinking because you were scared,' Crow suggested mildly.

The indifference vanished from his eyes to be replaced by a blur of caution, mingled with suspicion. Scales opened his mouth, then closed it again, twisting it in thought.

'What's that supposed to mean?' he said, with a rustle of menace in his voice.

Crow grunted, put his hands behind his back and looked down at the seated man.

'Pretty obvious, I would have thought. I interviewed James Klein a few days ago. He told me Donna Stark had been living with him but when he threw her out, about last March, she went back to you. Now then, let's look at the rest of it. She turns up in Wales, murdered. You turn up in Wales, drinking heavily after you've heard her body has been found. You say you're not saddened by her death. Isn't it logical to think you might be drinking to drown fears that the police might work out that you put her in the shaft?'

Scales jerked his hand spasmodically in an involuntary anger that he quickly controlled. He waited, chose his words with a care that would not have been possible minutes earlier, but the cold water and the questions had sobered him completely.

'I saw she was dead. I was sad. But not curious. Or scared. Nothing to do with me, any of it. We was finished, washed up.'

'When?'

'I told you. April.'

'A few minutes ago, it was May.'

Scales scowled at Dewi Jones, bit at his finger and said, 'Areet then, you want me to be accurate to the day. April, May, it was around then she and me parted. The exact date would be some time in third week of May, Because after I sailed on the *Isle of Arran* that was it. Never saw her again.'

Dewi Jones looked at Crow, knowing the importance of the next question.

'We'll be checking it,' Crow said softly, 'but by your recollection when was the date of sailing for your freighter?'

There was a jeering note in Scales's voice when he replied, almost as though he knew how he was about to torpedo their suspicions.

'May 29th, out of Cardiff and Barry. Check it till you're blue in the face.'

The room was silent. Crow and Jones looked at each other; they both knew what this meant and Scales would be foolish to give a date that could not be corroborated.

Crow sighed.

'All right. Mr Scales, that seems to let you out, since Mrs Stark was certainly in the Rhondda Valley after you left. But perhaps you'd be kind enough to help us further in our enquiries by answering a few more questions."

Scales rose and walked across the room to the washbasin. Underneath the basin was a crate. He pulled it out, took out the last bottle of beer and opened it. He grinned wolfishly at the two policemen.

'Ask away. What have I got to hide?'

* * *

The house was a quiet, semi-detached, unpretentious dwelling among the older premises behind Roath Park. It was fronted by a small stone wall that enclosed an unkempt square of turf edged with roses that were all but strangled by suckers. Crow looked at the roses sadly from where he sat with Jones in the car; he liked roses even though he had little time for gardening, and it was unfortunate those should have been allowed to grow like that.

It was well past midday and he and Jones had been waiting for an hour. The street had been quiet except for a few roundsmen and children coming home from the school at the far end of the street. If there was no sign of the man they were waiting for in the next twenty minutes Crow would have to leave the siege to Jones and go for lunch, before relieving Jones later.

'If he's out on a case,' Jones said with displeasure souring his voice, 'I hope she's been worth it. If you can't finish with a bird by midday. . .'

As if in answer a blue Morris came around the corner two hundred yards away. It drove sedately up towards them and parked outside the house with the dilapidated rose bushes. A man got out of the car, glanced casually towards them, locked the car and entered the house.

Crow and Jones got out of their car and walked to the house, knocked on the door, and the man who had entered opened it almost immediately. He had taken off his jacket and he carried it in his hand. He looked his two callers up and down and grinned in friendly fashion.

'Jacks if ever I saw one. You're looking for Teddy Skene?'

Crow nodded gravely.

'You've found him,' said the man in the doorway. 'And his house is yours because co-operation is and always has been Teddy Skene's watchword. Gentlemen, come in.'

He had wavy, thinning brown hair that was carefully arranged to hide the bare patches of scalp, and a stomach concealed by a carefully cut grey suit that had seen better days and would see worse. His nose was strong, his chin weak and his mouth was wide, smiling, friendly and co-operative. He would be a man who reacted to people; he reflected their moods faithfully, gave them what their words or their eyes told him they wanted, and in so doing he gave nothing of himself. He talked garrulously, but his garrulity was not uncontrolled — his verbal spasms were designed as carefully as his co-operation. If people like you, you can manipulate them. If you throw enough words at them they hear nothing—and they talk out of sheer necessity. It was why Crow said nothing while Skene spoke rapidly, machine-gunning his words and filling the room with the explosions.

'After all, the way I look at it, we're in much the same line of business. Sure enough, I don't look like a jack but what jack does, to an unpractised eye, unlike mine, I mean? I don't look like a jack, but then, I don't look like an enquiry agent either. I look like a butcher perhaps, or a clerk from town, or maybe even a bookie — at least when I wear that damned awful check suit of mine — but an enquiry agent, not likely! But that's all part of the business, isn't that so? I mean, when you fellers are working on a case you need to go about your business unobtrusively from time to time. You don't want to be spotted when you're waiting in a pub for a snout. Same with me. Not quite the same line but there are times when I'm in the dirty business, you know, followin' some chap's wife to see if she's sleeping with the milkman or whoever, and then what's there about me to notice? I mean, my suit? Not too good, not too scruffy. My appearance? What's there to remember about it? One of the reasons I went into the business, believe me, I just looked in the mirror one morning and I said, "Teddy, the gratuity's all but gone, what the hell you going to do now?" And the answer was there for me. Somethin' where being nondescript was useful; where being able to fade and merge was a good thing. So there it was . . .'

Dewi Jones did not possess Crow's patience and at last, with a hint of asperity, he cut in on Skene's chatter.

'If you just slow down a moment, Mr Skene, maybe we can explain why we're here.'

'Questions, ain't that it?' Skene smiled, showing two yellowing teeth and a gold-capped dog tooth. 'Jacks ask. But you should've told me you were coming, wouldn't have kept you waiting that way. Out of the way, on a case all night, it's a rough life—'

'Do you know Jack Scales?' Jones interrupted again.

'Jack? From way back. Hell, yes, we were old buddies.'

'It was he who put Donna Stark in touch with you?'

The effervescence faded somewhat, the mouth became tighter and less co-operative. Skene managed a smile, and scratched the lobe of his ear thoughtfully.

'Mrs Stark, is it? I wondered when you'd get around to me.'

'You remember her, then?'

Skene nodded.

'I remember her well enough. Wasn't all that long ago, after all, was it?'

He paused, as though expecting Dewi Jones to fill in the date for him; Jones did not. Instead, Crow said in a quiet voice, 'You remember her, and I assume you also know, probably from the Press, that her body was recently found in a mine shaft in the Rhondda. But you haven't contacted the police of your own accord.'

Skene hummed in his nose, waved his hands in front of him as though tossing a ball from one hand to another, and adopted a sly look, cocking his head on one side.

'Now, come on. You know the game as well as I do. Here I am, a private enquiry agent, wrong side of the door, isn't that so? You chaps don't like people like me, we're not legitimate. All right, so here I am, I get an assignment. I finish it and a few months later the bird turns up dead. Am I the one to go screaming to the police, 'I knew her, I knew her!' Am I hell! Oh, I guessed you'd finally make it to me because I got respect for you characters — you're a damned efficient lot. But equally, there was the chance you'd miss me, and if so, great. I mean, I'm being frank with you, you know? I don't want to get involved with any murder cases. You find me, I'm involved; I keep quiet, you don't find me, I'm not involved.'

'We found you,' Dewi Jones said.

'Yeah. I'm involved.'

'You'd better tell us how deeply,' Crow suggested.

Skene took a flat tin from his pocket, selected a miniature cigar and lit it. He puffed at the cigar for a few moments until its cheap aroma stained the air, and then he waved it theatrically in Crow's direction, jabbing it forward to emphasise his points.

'Involved yes; but deeply, not at all. A woman gets a recommendation to come see me, she comes, I do the job for her, purely investigative stuff, she goes away after paying up and I got no reason to go after her, never even see her again. Mrs Stark came in, and she went out. That was it. So I don't think you'll get much help from me.'

'What was the assignment she gave you?' Jones asked.

Skene affected mock astonishment.

'You surely don't expect me to tell you that! My relationship with my clients—'

'You won't get any clients unless you tell us all we want to know,' Jones said threateningly.

Skene grinned.

'I know it. But I had to make a gesture, hey? It was a search job. She wanted me to look up her long lost loved one. She wanted tags on her husband. . .the one that got away.'

'Her husband? Here in Cardiff?'

'So she thought.' Skene frowned suddenly, shook his head. 'Bloody hell, maybe I should have come to you rather than wait for you to find me. But the fact is, I didn't want to get involved in it all—'

He looked around the room blankly, as though realising for the first time that he was in his own sitting-room. The cheap paper-backed thrillers were stacked untidily in a glass-fronted bookcase, the settee cushions were stained and rumpled as though he had slept on them recently, and there was a dirty shirt hanging over the back of one of the chairs.

He walked across, twitched the shirt away and said, 'Let's sit down. Lemme get myself a drink and I'll stitch the whole thing together for you, start to finish.'

* * *

Once he started talking the cigar ash lengthened and the glow died. He talked quickly, smoothly, but once launched away from his preliminaries, by way of excuses and explanations once again for his silence, he kept pretty much to the point.

'To fill in the background, I better tell you about me and Jack Scales. I first met him in Cyprus. Okay, you look at me and my paunch now and you don't know – I was a PTI out in Cyprus and up to the neck in all that EOKA ruckus, almost got my head blown off a few times, but it was in a downtown bar that I came nearest to saying good night and then it was this big Navy character who lifted three wogs out through the window and got me free before the MPs arrived, and that was Jack Scales. Well, we saw a bit of each other after that, and when I left the Army and came home to Cardiff . . . well, I'm a Rhondda man, of course, but there's no good jobs up there, is there? Jack Scales rolled up one day too, off a ship, looked me up, we talked over old times, and during the last ten years it's happened a few times. Whenever he gets in at the docks, he looks me up. I got married eventually, coloured girl, smashing legs, but it didn't work out, and Jack drifted back north, Hartlepool, didn't see much of him. Then out of the blue, few months back, he turns up here again.'

Skene took a sip of his whisky, eyed the bottle as though he had little belief in the truth of its label, then continued.

'Now what I got to say from here on is part fact, part impression. But you've seen Jack Scales, you've heard his side of it and you'll be able to make up your mind whether what I say is right or wrong. But it seems to me the whole thing went something like this . . . When Jack Scales was up at Hartlepool he met this bird Donna Stark. This would be after she split from her old man, I reckon, but they shacked up together for a while because Jack had a fair bit of money at that time, and you got to admit he's a handsome chap when he takes the trouble to shave. 'Course, I don't know how they came to break, but my guess is Mrs Stark saw no long-term thing with Jack — I mean, he could give her a good time in more ways than one but she wanted a bit of cash as well, so after a while she pushed off. Jack told me she went to live with a bloke called Klein . . . though there was something funny about that, Jack hinted she was pressuring Klein about something . . . and it was a good time after that she suddenly returned to Jack.'

Skene looked at his cigar disgustedly, ground its tip into an ashtray on the table and wrapped his fingers around his glass again as though warming them.

'Now it could be she left Klein of her own accord, could be she was thrown out. But Jack was certainly no good to her. He was fed up with the north, he was thinking of going back to sea, and though he said that was the reason he brought her to me I don't think it really went like that. I don't reckon Mrs Stark even thought of sticking to Jack; she was just using him. And she used him to good effect. He gave her a bed for a few weeks and then, when she got started on the hunt for her old man, he was able to put her in touch with me.'

'Why you?' Crow asked coldly.

For a moment Skene didn't like it and allowed the feeling to show. He brushed it away with a grin, part cynical, part indulgent.

'Ha, you jacks, you're all the same. You're the professionals, you don't see any mileage in us fellers beyond the door. Well, let me tell you, I get my days! But, fair enough, why me? The answer comes in two packets: Donna Stark knew her husband had moved then south to Newcastle before she shacked up with Jack and then Klein, and she had a feeling it'd be Cardiff, Wales, somewhere around here; second, Jack Scales was thinking if she wasn't staying he could take a freighter from the Docks down here and do her the favour she wanted as well. . .*he* couldn't find her old man for her and didn't want to anyway, but he could put her in touch with a friend who possessed the necessary skills.'

'Teddy Skene,' Dewi Jones said grimly.

'The one and only.' Skene grinned again, tapped his whisky glass against his teeth. 'And that's how it was. Jack had a word with me, squared things, brought Donna Stark around and I was given the assignment. It took me three weeks, she paid up once I gave her the information, and that was that.'

His grin had gone and was now replaced with a foxy smile as he looked from one policeman to the other.

'All this square with what Jack told you?'

'More or less,' Crow said. 'But there's still a few questions.'

'Lemme answer them before you ask,' Skene said swiftly. 'First, Jack pushed off, went to sea, I didn't see him for several months, just recently, matter of fact. Second, I didn't see all that much of Donna Stark. She visited me three times: one, to give me what she had by way of facts; two, to check on how things were going; three, to get the goods and pay up. And when she paid, she was on her uppers.'

Crow frowned.

'How do you mean?'

'I mean she was ten quid short. I could have quibbled, maybe asked for it in kind, but I don't work that racket, it's the way coal bills don't get paid, you know? But I gave her what she wanted, she paid me what she could, and she went. Last I saw of her.'

'When was this?'

Skene screwed up his eyes as though thinking hard, though Crow guessed it was a mere pretence; Skene would have known exactly what he was going to say the moment the police walked into his house. He was no fool, he had guessed they'd reach him eventually, he would have worked at his memory to get all the facts straight, supportable, and beyond doubt.

'June . . . fifth, I reckon.'

'You're precise.'

'On the sixth I tangled with a lascar down in Bute Street; late evening, I was shadowing this bird and the lascar came out, left most of his upper plate in my knuckle when I hit him. I'm short-tempered for an enquiry agent—someone comes at me, I hit him first, think things over later.'

'Not a good way to live,' Dewi Jones rumbled.

'But I'm still alive — and after Cyprus and Cardiff Docks that's saying something,' Skene replied swiftly.

'All right,' Crow said, 'you gave Mrs Stark her information on the fifth of June and she left.'

'Never saw her again, or heard of her till I read about the body in the Bwylffa. Then I closed my mouth and waited for you. But I'll tell you one thing, without you asking. I know what she wanted from her old man"

'What was that?'

'Money, of course.' Skene grinned, and satisfaction marked his tones with an unpleasant sound. 'I seen it in women before, and it was there in her face. She intended soaking her old man when she got her hands on him, it was there in her mouth, and it was there in her eyes. She had hard eyes, but maybe experience had done that for her. And one thing more; it's my guess he wasn't going to like her asking, either. That was in her face too . . . she was eager to soak him, but she was not far from scared, either. Excited scared, you know what I mean? Nervy.'

The two policemen sat silently for a while. Crow thought about the dead woman in the shaft and how she had appeared the last time Skene had seen her. Excited, nervy, intense with the thought that she needed to gear herself up to demand money from her husband, the man who had left her . . . or had been deserted? . . .

'The word is blackmail, I think,' Skene said abruptly.

Crow was surprised. There was a nervous undercurrent in Skene's voice that affected him like an electric charge and once he had spoken Skene seemed to regret it.

'On what grounds would she try to extort money?' Crow asked.

Skene shrugged.

'You'd have to ask him; I wouldn't know.'

'But you do know where we can find him?'

'That was the information she came to me for,' Skene began to rise, turning towards the door. 'But I'd have to go take a look at my files to—'

'No,' Crow said. 'You don't need to look at any files. You've already checked, against the day we came here. Where will we find him?'

Skene stood still. His face was suddenly greyer, as though conscious of the fact he should have come forward earlier with the information and now a little scared at the likely repercussions for his silence.

'In the Rhondda.'

He hesitated and then, with a subdued pride in his work struggling through to reassert itself beneath the anxiety, he added, 'But it wasn't easy, believe me. She came to me, told me her husband was called Stark, had Welsh connections, had come south probably to Wales, was a solicitor, and I tell you, I checked every bloody where. And if he hadn't been fool enough to take a job which had legal connections I'd never have found him, even then.'

'How do you mean?'

'You see, when he came to Wales he threw over his membership of the Law Society, or maybe he got removed from the Roll, I don't know. You'll have to check that out for yourselves: I didn't look into it. But he had legal knowledge, and he was a professional man, and there was one way he could make a good living without ever having to join a professional body. And that's what he did. But he still had contacts with lawyers. And that was how I got him, in the end. I showed the photograph Mrs Stark had given me to God knows how many solicitors and at last, in the Cardiff Arms Hotel of all places, up in Treorchy, I hit the jackpot. A solicitor from the Rhondda, he was with the chap I was talking to, he looked over his shoulder, saw the snapshot and said he knew him. Not a lawyer, he said, but he'd had dealings with him. Not a lawyer, and not called Stark. But the same chap, right enough.'

Skene paused as though for effect, awaiting approval.

Crow sat woodenly, unwilling to give Skene his little triumph.

Disappointedly, Skene grunted.

'Not a lawyer. An estate agent up in the Rhondda. In Pentre. Martin Evans.'

* * *

Ceinwen Williams tapped on the door and opened it. There was a slight frown on her face as though she were facing something she should know about but did not. Martin Evans looked up from the papers he had spread in front of him in his office.

'Two gentlemen to see you,' Ceinwen said. 'Policemen.'

It was no question, but the query was there in her voice. Martin Evans looked stolidly at her, expressionless.

'Detective Chief Inspector Crow and Detective Inspector Jones,' Ceinwen said as though reciting a Sunday school litany. Something flickered in Martin Evans's features but it was gone before she could seize on it, identify it as an emotion.

'Shall I let them in?'

For a moment she thought he was not going to answer. She opened her mouth. 'Martin, it can't be—'

'No,' he said quickly. 'Show them in, Ceinwen. And. . . and after you've done that, go home.'

Puzzled, she stared at him as though she could not believe what she had heard.

'*Go home*, Ceinwen,' he repeated, and his tone was final.

As she retreated, bewildered and anxious, Crow appeared behind her. He leaned forward.

'It's possible we may wish to ask a few questions of Miss Williams.'

Martin Evans placed his hands on the table in front of him and looked directly at Crow. 'I don't think it will be necessary,' he said.

The message in his eyes was unmistakable. Strain marked his features and it was obvious to Crow that Martin Evans had been expecting a visit from the police for some time. More than that, he had reached the point where he no longer wished to hide, or prevaricate, or deny. Martin Evans was vulnerable. Crow didn't like it. He preferred to deal with men who had a certain amount of iron in them, so that he could push for the truth without compunction. When a man was near breaking point, as Martin Evans was, there was always the danger that sympathy broke through in Crow's attitudes.

This was dangerous, for all the layers might not then get peeled away.

Crow walked into the room, Dewi Jones just behind him. Jones closed the door quietly, then stood with his back to it. He obviously expected John Crow to undertake the questioning but this Crow was reluctant to do immediately.

He wanted to watch Martin Evans. He looked towards Dewi Jones, nodded, then walked towards the window, glanced out at the hillside, then turned to face Martin Evans.

'Inspector Jones has some questions for you, Mr Evans.'

Evans sat very still, saying nothing. His grey eyes were blank, and his craggy features seemed to have crumbled like rain-rotted rock. He was withdrawing into himself; it was as though he would be listening to their words from a distance. Crow had seen this before: a man unwilling to face reality and the horror of truth, but forced to come to grips with it by the very predicament in which he found himself.

Dewi Jones cleared his throat, marched forward, took a chair, sat down, and pulled out a pencil and notebook.

'Mr Evans, you are the owner of this business, Morgan and Enoch, Estate Agents?'

The grey eyes were unwavering but Evans nodded slightly.

'Before you bought the business, and came to live here, where were you living and what were you doing?'

There was no reply. Dewi Jones frowned, waited for a brief period, bit his lip thoughtfully, glanced towards Crow and then tried again.

'Was it from Newcastle you came?'

Martin Evans remained silent, but there was a flicker in his eyes.

'We think you were up in Newcastle. What were you doing there?'

Still there was no reply. Evans sat motionless and Dewi Jones stirred uncomfortably in his chair. Irritation entered his tones.

'Now come on, man, it's no good just sitting there saying nothing. We've got a job to do, this is a murder enquiry, we got questions to ask, and if you're not willing to answer them here, you know you'll just have to come down to the station in Tonypandy with us and answer them there. So see sense, man, cooperate with us a bit and let's get things straightened out.'

Evans blinked several times, as though trying to get rid of a mist before his eyes, but he still seemed unable to focus properly on Jones. Crow frowned, looked over his shoulder towards the hillside again. The top of the winding house at the Bwylffa was just visible, stark against the backdrop of the mountain.

Quietly, Crow said, 'You'd have been able to see what was happening up on the hill, there at the pit when they discovered the body, wouldn't you?'

Perhaps it was the contrast between Jones's voice and Crow's; perhaps it was the change of tack, the reference to the hill. Whatever it was, it reached Martin Evans. He looked at Crow and the window beyond; his eyes cleared, his mouth opened, and though he said nothing at least he was alert again. Crow suddenly felt very sorry for this man, for he was beginning to see how it all could have happened.

'We know your name is Stark,' he said abruptly.

Martin Evans seemed in no way surprised. He stared at Crow levelly, as though summing him up, and then in a voice remarkably controlled in view of his earlier state of shock he said, 'Perhaps it would be sensible to tell me what else you know"

He had not been surprised; Crow was. The reaction was not what he had expected and he was puzzled.

'That's not the way to proceed,' he suggested. 'We're here to ask questions so it would be better if you told us all about what happened up there.'

Martin Evans smiled thinly. He seemed to be growing in confidence suddenly, as though he had reached a decision.

'That's an old trick,' he said. 'Remember, I was a lawyer. An old trick, get me to make admissions, suggest to me you know lots of things whereas you really know nothing. It won't do. You ask questions, I'll try answers in so far as I wish to answer. You're right so far, I'll admit that. My real name, the one I was baptised with, was Martin Stark. I changed it when I came to live here in the Rhondda.'

'Why?'

'A man can change his surname if he wishes; his Christian name, no, for it's the name he has given to God—'

'Are you a religious man, Mr Stark?' Crow asked.

Martin paused for a moment, then shook his head. 'I would rather you didn't use my previous surname. Now, I'm Martin Evans. As for religion . . . I believed. I no longer do so. I cannot accept that God would allow . . . what he allows to happen. As for using the name Evans. It's the name I adopted out of choice. Stark. . . that's something I've put behind me.'

'Because of the trouble you got into under that name?' Dewi Jones asked quickly.

Martin Evans turned to look at him in the same level, calculating way he had stared at Crow, as though measuring his enemies, seeking out their strengths and weaknesses.

'What trouble?' he asked, and his voice was calm and controlled.

Jones was annoyed at the response; perhaps he had expected Martin Evans to give way more easily in view of his attitude when they had entered, and an edge crept into his tone. Crow was on the point of interrupting him, cooling him so that he did not give too much away, but then he checked himself for he was still curious about Martin Evans. He allowed Dewi Jones to continue, and Jones showed his inexperience immediately.

'Come off it, Evans, we know all about what went on! We've been making enquiries in the north-east, and in Cardiff, and we've managed to paint the picture ourselves without reference to you. We know exactly what happened, and why.'

'If you already know it all, how can I help you?' Evans asked coldly.

'By telling us *why* you killed your wife!' Jones replied snappishly. Suddenly aware he was losing his temper he looked guiltily at Crow, but Crow was staring at the floor.

'My wife,' Evans repeated.

'Donna Stark. The woman we found in the shaft. The shaft you can see from this office, the shaft where you dumped her when she came here blackmailing you!'

Evans moved involuntarily, his fingers suddenly tensing on the table top. There was a harder line to his mouth.

'You're making wild statements. Not questions. I don't have to listen to this,' he said in a harsh voice.

'You bloody well do,' Jones replied, reacting to Evans with a further spasm of anger. 'Stop pussyfooting around for God's sake and let's get this over with. We've got plenty of facts, enough to piece the whole thing together. You were employed in the north-east by a firm of solicitors and you got married to a woman who was looking out for the main chance. She was working as a clerk in the same office, she hooked you, and it was only after you were married that you realised what she was really like — far from virginal and a bitch as well. All right, things didn't work out, but that might have been bearable, but it wasn't bearable when she landed you in the cart with your employers, was it?'

'You're behaving in an unprofessional manner,' Martin Evans said bitterly. 'Accusations such as these require no answer from me!'

'You don't have to admit anything! We've got enough damned witnesses to fit it all together! Your firm was involved in a fraud case — you were acting for Northeast Credit. Some papers came into your possession relating to James Klein; your marriage was going on the rocks, and Donna, your wife, was already thinking of leaving, even if you weren't. But she needed cash, so she extracted those papers and sold them to Klein — which got him off the hook — and then she left you and went to live with a man called Scales. A big, handsome lad, but when the money ran out she turned back to Klein. We think she tried to blackmail him, that we'll find out, but the fact is she ended up living with him. It suited them both. But you. . . you were no longer around. You pushed off — or were given the push, and you started a new life here in the Rhondda. You buried yourself, for good, you hoped.'

Jones paused, uncertain suddenly. He looked at Crow, and the Chief Inspector nodded. His eyes were fixed on Evans.

'You built up this business,' Jones continued, 'and things were going well. A quiet life. But things weren't quiet for Donna Stark. Klein had found another woman, one he wanted to marry. So he gave Donna the push. She went to Scales, but he was just a seaman. What about Martin? She asked herself the question, decided to look you up, get some money out of you. She came to Cardiff with Scales, engaged an enquiry agent called Skene, and he traced you. Then . . .'

Martin Evans was drifting again, his eyes clouded with unpleasant memories. He fought them off, held them at bay and glared at Jones, concentrating.

'Then what?'

'You tell us.'

Evans grimaced, drummed his fingers on the table. His uncertainty had returned completely now, he was nervous and unsettled.

'You say you know it all. Why stop there? What other facts do you have? It's just supposition. . .Why should I tell you anything at all?'

'We can make a guess,' Jones said. 'We know she was after money. Maybe she came here and told you she'd expose you in the Rhondda, make it known you'd been thrown out of the legal profession for suspicion of fraud and theft. And in anger you attacked her, killed her, by accident maybe, dragged her up to the pit head, hid her body in the shaft. . .'

Evans twisted in his chair, staring at his hands, quiescent again on the table top.

'Hardly a motive for murder, fear of being exposed in that way.'

Jones grunted.

'The valley being what it is, gossip rife, everyone living in everybody's pocket, the fingers would have pointed, your business would have gone down the drain, for the second time your life would have been destroyed.'

His voice died away, for Evans had lapsed into the same state he had been in when they first came to the office. His glance was vacant, his mouth loose, his whole personality had backed away like a cat from a snarling dog, and it was as though he were no longer with them. He was lost in the contemplation of his own past and the strain in his face told them the memories were far from happy ones. The silence grew around them, deepened, became almost tangible as a light sheen of sweat gathered on Martin Evans's brow and Crow and Jones waited.

The silence began to affect Dewi Jones; he shuffled in his seat and looked to Crow for some sort of guidance, but Crow shook his head without speaking. Something was happening to Martin Evans, decisions were being reached inside his head and the repercussions were marking his face with pain. Crow was puzzled, curious and in an odd way alarmed.

It was like watching a man prepare himself for a watershed in his life, knowingly, understanding that he had much to lose and nothing to gain but loneliness and death. It was beyond Crow's experience, this long, agonized silence, and it was something he could not measure or evaluate. He was too close to it, and too close to Evans, physically and emotionally. To recall it later, away from the man and the time, this might bring answers to him, but now none were possible.

But at last Martin Evans moved. He sighed lightly and his mouth tightened, hardened into a determined line. Crow stood away from the window. Dewi Jones was startled, caught Crow's nod, failed to comprehend it for a moment and then understood.

'Martin Evans,' he said quickly. 'I want you to understand that you may make a statement if you wish but you are under no obligation to do so. If you do make a statement it is voluntary, and given under no threat or promise from us. But any statement you make, it may later be used in evidence if you wish to speak at this time.'

Martin Evans raised his head. His craggy features expressed the confidence of a man who knows he is doing right.

'As a matter of procedure, it would have been more satisfactory had you said that earlier. No matter. It's as you said it was. I admit it. Donna Stark was my wife. It was she who took those papers relating to Klein though I couldn't prove it. I was suspected of collusion, and was asked to leave the partnership. Rather than face an enquiry at the Law Society I came down here to the Rhondda, started this estate agency and put it on its feet. Then she turned up again . . .'

'When?' Crow asked quickly.

'June. The date . . .'

He hesitated and Jones said, 'The sixth?'

Crow subdued the feeling of annoyance at the foolish interruption from Dewi Jones as Martin Evans nodded.

'Yes. That would be it, She phoned me, said she wanted to see me. I could guess that she would be wanting money, would interfere with my life, would threaten me. I didn't want our meeting to be public, so we arranged to meet on the track behind the office. From there we walked up to the old pit, stood arguing. She told me she wanted money. I got angry. She threatened me. We were standing near the wheelhouse. I lost my temper. I hit her, shouted at her, hit her again when she flailed at me. She fell into the wheelhouse.'

He seemed very calm, almost detached as he spoke.

* * *

'And what would your advice be, Chief Inspector Crow? We have all the facts. We have witnesses who will testify as to what happened before the sixth of June, it all ties in, and to cap it all we have Martin Evans's confession.'

Crow faced the Chief Constable and the Chief Superintendent coolly.

'The case *looks* a reasonably strong one, but I would advise caution, sir. The confession is crucial, for we have no witnesses as to the act itself, or as to the meeting between husband and wife. So if the defence should attack the confession—'

'It looks pretty watertight to me,' the Chief Superintendent said.

'I'd counsel caution, sir,' Crow said doggedly. 'Further investigation . . .'

'Is unnecessary, in my view.' The Chief Constable heaved a sigh. 'We've appreciated your co-operation and your assistance, Chief Inspector Crow. I'm sure the Murder Squad has plenty on its plate not to want you to spend more time with us in Wales. I feel now we can offer thanks and allow you to return to your usual duties.'

'There are still a few points, sir,' Crow insisted, 'a few points that need clearing up. Times and dates—'

'We can see to that.'

'And the letter. . .or rather the envelope without a letter in his desk—'

'You suggest its presence demands explanation and Evans will give none. A red herring, Crow, the suggestion of blackmail will hardly stand up. I mean, after all, an envelope with crudely printed block capitals, the fact Evans denies knowing anything about it, I don't see it has any bearing on the case. We can safely disregard it.'

'There are other matters, sir. His demeanour when he was questioned by Inspector Jones, the motive behind the killing of the woman, these are matters I'm not very satisfied about. All I'm saying now is, not that I believe Evans is not telling the truth, but he's not telling us *all* the truth. There's the possibility that if you take this case to court now it will not be adequately prepared.'

Crow hesitated as he saw the thunderclouds gather on the Chief Constable's brow. Quickly, he added, 'There's the chance we might be prosecuting before we have all the facts, and if there are any loopholes, if the confession obtained is subjected to a fierce attack by defence counsel, if—'

'What is your advice, Chief Inspector? Succinctly, please.'

Crow's voice became quieter, a sign of his own anger at the cutting edge in the Chief Constable's tone.

‘I advise caution, sir. I advise against immediate prosecution. I advise further investigation. I suggest a request that Martin Evans be held pending such further enquiries—’

‘No magistrate would accept it,’ the Chief Constable snapped. ‘Either we have a case or we don’t. We’ve arrested him, we have a case. Further delay is pointless. We thank you, Chief Inspector. You’ve given us much valuable assistance. But your position was, by prior agreement, an advisory and consultative one. You have advised us; we have consulted you.’

He gathered up the papers in front of him.

‘The decision whether to proceed must be ours, after due consultation with the Director of Public Prosecutions.’

CHAPTER 5

Commander Gray was displeased by the suggestion but John Crow pressed his arguments with force. In the first instance, if it became absolutely necessary, Crow would simply take a backlog of leave due to him and spend it in Cardiff. But secondly, there were other considerations to take into account: the fact that the Murder Squad was not overstretched at this particular time. Crow himself had recently undertaken two investigations that had been rapidly concluded, and it was necessary to send a representative to the forensic science conference at the University of Wales. The third argument was perhaps the most cogent, however, and most likely to appeal to Commander Gray: a chief inspector of the Murder Squad had been attached to the investigation into the murder of Donna Stark, his duties had been advisory and consultative, he had counselled caution and his advice had been disregarded. There were two possibilities therefore — the case against Martin Evans might stagger to an unsuccessful conclusion, and the involvement of the Murder Squad might be seen to be utterly ineffective.

It was the last possibility Commander Gray was not happy about. He was a political animal in his bones, he obeyed his masters. So when Crow suggested the solution he finally agreed: John Crow should be the representative selected to attend the conference at the University of Wales, but should at the same time hold a watching brief on the preliminary hearing before the magistrates in the matter of the prosecution of Martin Evans.

'I suppose you have doubts about his guilt,' Gray said sourly.

'Not exactly. I just think we don't know the whole story. And you know as well as I do that if the ends aren't all completely tied up it might get thrown out as no case to answer, or worse, it might get to the Crown Court and fail badly there. Reputations can be lost . . .'

It was enough for Gray.

* * *

John Crow attended the sherry party at the conference, though he did not care for such forced occasions, then took dinner with the rest of the members. He sat in on the first lecture, in which an eminent pathologist spoke of the use of body temperature in estimating the time of death, and the limitations to be recognized in the evidential value of the pathologist's deductions. In his room later that night John Crow found himself staring at and not understanding the exponential terms he had written in his notebook '*where O : the temperature excess of the rectum over the environment at the time t and B, C, Z, p= constants for the corpse under observation. . .*'

He found great difficulty in going to sleep that night, the words *constants for the corpse under observation* spinning around in his mind until they somehow became utterly confused with Martin Evans and Donna Stark and a deep black shaft. The shaft became his room at four in the morning, the distant wail of an ambulance siren was

Donna Stark's death cry, and Martin Evans was the enigma, the dark shadow in the darkness.

Constants.

What had been the constants in Martin Evans's case? The interview with Evans, the man's vagueness and then resolution, his firmness in confession . . .

The lecture for the morning concerned inaccuracy and under-reporting in certification of death. Crow decided to give it a miss, go back up to the Rhondda and attend the magistrates court for the preliminary hearing. He still puzzled over the thought that there were no 'constants' in Martin Evans. It was the thing that had bothered John Crow from the beginning, but only now was it becoming obvious. When Crow and Dewi Jones had spoken to Evans he had reacted, but his reactions had changed: he had wanted information, he had given little, he had accepted facts and built a confession around those. But what if the basis of those facts could be challenged?

What was the constant factor in the conduct of Martin Evans? Crow was beginning to hazard a guess.

The courtroom was crowded, as he might have supposed, but when he identified himself a place was made available for him. He soon had reason to be thankful for the Chief Constable's decision not to use Crow as a witness but to rely instead upon his own men. The prosecuting counsel was a man unknown to Crow: his name was Weir, he was a dark-faced Welshman with eloquent hands and he had already outlined the case for the prosecution the day before.

Some witnesses had already been examined, and evidence of the marriage between Martin Evans and Donna had already been adduced. During the session James Klein was called to the witness-box, and Crow paid little attention to his evidence as he was taken through his story relating to Donna Stark living with him, then leaving to join Jack Scales. Instead of listening, Crow kept his eyes on Martin Evans, watching him carefully.

He was cool. He was dressed in a dark grey suit and his face was expressionless. He barely moved as Klein went through his evidence and he stared straight ahead of him. Crow watched and wondered. Constant factors . . . constancy . . .

Counsel for Martin Evans was rising to his feet. Crow knew him and felt a quiver of involuntary excitement and apprehension. Jason Warlock had made himself a reputation with witnesses, judges and opposing counsel: he was six feet tall, with fair hair and a slight stoop that had been uncorrected in spite of his time in the Brigade of Guards. Warlock was well known for his acid comments, his penetrating cross-examinations, and his skill in legal niceties. He was unloved, efficient, clinical and contemptuous of those who did not reach his own standards. But, above all, he was thorough.

He began quietly enough by getting Klein to stress some of the points already made. Klein was at ease, elegant in a cream shirt and brown tie, shoulders back and head up, conscious of his good looks and the impression of solidity and confidence his deep resonant voice made. Nevertheless, his confidence was shaken somewhat when Warlock suddenly asked,

'Tell me about Northeast Credit, Mr Klein., '

'I. . .I'm sorry. . .'

Warlock arched a contemptuous eyebrow.

'Surely the request is straightforward? I want you to tell me about this firm. Northeast Credit were mentioned as your employers in examination-in-chief so my learned friend can have no objection. Why did you leave the firm, Mr Klein?'

'It closed down,' Klein answered stiffly.

'For what reason?'

'It just went out of business.'

'Because of your frauds?'

The prosecuting attorney rose to his feet quickly.

'Your honour, we really cannot allow—'

Warlock held up an imperious hand.

'The question is withdrawn. My apologies to the court: the question slipped out. I shall rephrase it. Were you questioned by the police in connection with frauds perpetrated at Northeast Credit?'

Klein grimaced, drawing his lips back over his teeth. 'I was, but—'

'No proceedings were taken because of lack of documentary evidence.'

'There was no evidence,' Klein snapped.

'No? Did not a solicitor representing the firm collect certain documents from the office one month before the investigations began? Did not those documents later disappear? Was not the solicitor in question the accused, Martin Evans?'

James Klein was pale, his self-assurance gone, and he looked helplessly towards Weir. The prosecuting counsel rose to his defence, protesting that he saw no point in this line of questioning, but both he and Crow knew exactly what Warlock was up to. James Klein was a leading witness for the prosecution: he had testified as to the fact of the break-up of the marriage between Martin and Donna Stark, the fact of Donna Stark's character, her rejection by James Klein and her consequent seeking out of her husband with a view to extracting money from him. He had laid a foundation upon which other witnesses would build, consequentially. Warlock was out to shake the solidity of that base.

'There is more to all this than has come out in James Klein's testimony,' Warlock was arguing with cold passion in response to the objections raised. 'He has given us facts, but I wish to be clear as to motivations. Why did Donna Stark leave her husband? How was it that she found James Klein so ready to take her in? If she was so ready to blackmail her husband, had she already blackmailed James Klein? Was she blackmailing James Klein? He had a great deal to lose. The prosecution is arguing that Martin Evans had a motive in wanting to murder his wife. Was he alone in this?'

He turned swiftly, facing James Klein once more.

'Where were you on June 6th, Mr Klein?'

Klein licked his lips.

'I was on a business trip, in London, but I'm not here to answer questions on —'

'You'll answer such questions as I put, Mr Klein,' Warlock said tigerishly, 'and I intend putting questions as to your credit as a witness.'

And he did. Crow knew Warlock, had heard him before, but he marvelled at the skilful way in which Warlock skated on the edge of acceptability in the questions he put to Klein. But at the end of the day it became apparent that he had done all he had set out to do: James Klein's testimony still stood, but Klein himself had been branded as a man of shady background and doubtful virtue, a man involved, possibly in fraud, if not something worse, an amoral, self-centred man whose reputation was worth little and whose word was worth less.

It was quite a performance.

When it was over Crow left, returned to Cardiff and sat in on a lecture at the University on hormonal treatment for sexual offenders.

* * *

The following day Crow found himself embroiled in a discussion group at the conference and was unable to escape until mid-afternoon to return to the Rhondda. As he entered the magistrates' court he caught sight of Detective-Inspector Dewi Jones and he called his name. Jones turned, smiled, seemed pleased to see Crow. He was clearly less pleased about the course of the preliminary investigation.

'Anyone would think it was a full-scale trial in there! Who does this chap Warlock think he is, anyway? All right, have a go at the prosecution witnesses, but this man, hey, he's grilling them like trout over an open fire.'

'It's my guess he'll want to suggest to the magistrates there's no case to answer,' Crow said.

Dewi Jones pulled a face.

'Don't see much chance of that coming off. We got the evidence, after all, haven't we?'

'That may be, I'm not sure. What do you think about Martin Evans?'

'Taking it calm, isn't he? Mind you, he's been the same ever since we took him into custody.' Jones fingered his lip thoughtfully. 'You were never very happy about it all, were you?'

Crow pursed his lips.

'Well, let's put it like this. There are aspects of the case I'm not too pleased about. Did you ever manage to find any more about that envelope in Evans's desk?'

'The one with the printed address?' Jones shook his head. 'We asked the girl, Ceinwen Williams, about it, but she reckoned she'd never seen it at all, let alone the contents of the letter it might have contained. The Chief Super was inclined to shrug it off anyway, since he couldn't see where it would conceivably fit in the case he had made out against Evans.'

Crow understood. The Chief Superintendent was not alone in his attitude. There were many policemen who either started a case with preconceived ideas, or else formulated opinions during the course of an investigation, and then refused to be moved from the conclusion they had reached. Thereafter, it would be a situation where evidence was selected to fit a point of view: if it fitted the theory, it was acceptable; if it did not fit, it was rejected as irrelevant.

'Who are the witnesses to be called after this?' Crow asked.

'That fellow Scales is giving evidence this afternoon,' Jones replied. 'After him, the enquiry agent Skene will be called, then Dai Davies, the fish-and-chip merchant. I'll be ending up with the confession. I've got to admit, the way Warlock handled Klein, I'm not too happy about the prospect of facing him with the confession.'

Crow had sympathy with Jones's point of view. It would be crucial to Warlock to upset that confession, but for that matter Crow had been uneasy about it all along. Evans's capitulation disturbed him . . . it was a matter of constants again. Evans had vacillated in his attitudes that day, indifference, vagueness, nervous excitement, and finally capitulation. It hadn't been skill on Jones's part that had drawn out the confession. It had been freely given, without a great deal of pressure being applied. It bothered Crow.

Jack Scales was being bothered by Jason Warlock, Crow found, when he took a seat in court.

'I think you will have to explain this rather more clearly for my benefit,' Warlock was saying sarcastically. 'I find it difficult to understand just why Mrs Stark came looking for *you*. So recap for me, please. When you first lived with her what were your financial circumstances?'

'I had a fair bit of money stashed away,' Scales said grudgingly. 'Not a lot, but enough to spend about a bit, give her a good time.'

'But this was shortly after she had left her husband, and he had left the area?'

'Yes.'

'But did you not already state, when questioned by my learned friend, that she herself had "a fair bit of cash"?'

Scales was somewhat flustered. He turned his handsome head towards Weir helplessly, but there was no assistance from that direction. Weir's head was down, as he read his notes.

'Well, yes, she did have a fair bit. I never asked where she got it from —'

'Not her husband, surely?'

'Well, no,'

'From James Klein, as payment for the documents abstracted from Evans's office?'

Weir began to rise, again in protest.

Warlock waved his hand, stopped both the complaint from Weir and the answer from Scales, and continued, 'All right, she had money. Why then did she come to you? Merely for sexual satisfaction?'

Scales didn't like the sneer in the comment. He stood stiffly, his eyes angry.

'I gave her a good time. I treated her right.'

'You lived together.'

'Yes.'

'Your sexual life with her was satisfactory.'

'She didn't complain.'

Warlock nodded, his eyes glittering. 'But she left you and went to live with Klein. Why?'

'The money ran out.'

'So what was it she was after?' Warlock asked swiftly. 'Sex or money?'

'From me, both,' Scales replied angrily. 'From Klein . . .' He stopped and Warlock smiled wolfishly.

'From Klein . . ?' he prompted gently.

'I think that was more of a business arrangement. From Klein, she wanted . . . she wanted money. I think she pressured Klein, but she was a good-looking woman, and Klein . . . well, I think he said he'd pay her but she had to give as well as keep quiet. So they lived together.'

'I see . . .' Warlock consulted his notes, smiling thinly. 'But the second time she came to you, what did she want then? The same combination? Sex? Money? What *was* it she was after?'

Scales shook his head.

'You got it wrong! It wasn't like that. Klein threw her out. She told me she had threatened to spill the truth about the frauds but he was past caring, he said she'd only be involving herself anyway and she was bluffing. I guess she was. You got to remember, Donna was hard, but she didn't have much by way of guts. She wanted the easy way all the time. It was too much trouble to fight Klein once she saw his mind was made up. She clawed him then she came to me. We had sex, sure, but I reckon she came to me more for friendship—'

'*Friendship*?' Warlock's tone was cutting.

'Friendship and help,' Scales repeated stubbornly. 'She wanted to find her husband again.'

'Why?'

'To put the squeeze on him. She'd tried that game with Klein and it had paid off for a while until Klein threw her out. She decided she'd go after her old man, try it again with him.'

'And you helped her . . . by taking her to Cardiff to see an enquiry agent.'

Scales nodded.

'That was the end of it for me. We split up then.'

'You mean she'd had enough sex . . . sorry, *friendship* and assistance?'

Scales flushed, angry at the open contempt in Warlock's tone.

'We quarrelled. She knew I didn't want to be stuck with her. That was one reason why she was after her husband. I had no cash; I wanted to go back to sea; I couldn't give her what she wanted.'

'What was that?'

'I already said. Money. Security, I suppose. Donna had an awful fear of growing old and ending up in the gutter.'

Warlock nodded.

'So you passed her to an enquiry agent . . .' He shuffled the papers in front of him, then almost casually, asked, 'Did you love Donna Stark?'

Scales hesitated, considered the word 'love' as though it were strange to him, then shrugged.

'I was fond of her. I suppose at one time I did love her.'

Jason Warlock wrinkled his nose, nodded and then spoke carefully. 'Let me put a case to you, Mr Scales. Imagine this: a woman leaves her husband and takes up a new life with her lover. She then leaves the lover to live with someone else but later returns to him. When she finds he cannot give her the security she wants she decides to leave him a second time and return to her husband. What would that lover do?'

'I don't follow,' Scales said, but there was a shakiness in his voice that suggested he knew very well the direction in which Warlock was headed.

'I'll spell it out slowly,' Warlock said in a silky tone. 'That lover could have felt angry; he could have wanted to do something about it; he could have argued with her after she had found her husband; he could have pleaded for her to stay with him, wait until he had returned from sea. Maybe she refused. Maybe in a fit of passion he—'

'It never happened,' Scales interrupted, and his voice rose as he leaned forward and gripped the edge of the witness box. 'It wasn't like that. I didn't love her, didn't want her, I handed her over to Teddy Skene and was glad to see the back of her. She was trouble, always was; me, Stark, Klein, she was trouble for all of us. But I'd finished with her, it wasn't the way you say. I went to sea—'

'Ah yes.' Warlock held up his hand, stopping Scales's nervous flow of speech. 'You went to sea. The freighter . . .?'

'Isle of Arran.'

'Ah yes, that's right. *Isle of Arran.* The freighter that left Cardiff Docks on . . . when was it exactly?'

'May 29th.'

'And stopped off in Barry Dock?'

'That's so. We finally left on June 2nd, as far as I remember.'

'As far as you remember .' Warlock smiled unpleasantly. 'No doubt you'll also remember the date given as to the likely death of Mrs Stark?'

'June 6th,' Scales snapped out.

'As far as you remember . . . So you sailed on May 29th, June 2nd, and Mrs Stark died on June 6th . . . are these the facts as you remember then?'

'Yes.'

Warlock consulted the papers in front of him, frowning as though puzzled. Mildly, wonderingly, he said, 'As far as I've been able to ascertain the *Isle of Arran* . . . that was your freighter, yes? . . . she left Barry Docks on the 12th June. How can you explain this apparent discrepancy in your evidence? I should add I have the dock schedules to support this statement.'

Scales stood still. The colour ebbed from his face and his eyes were glaring. From where he sat Crow could see Weir, prosecuting counsel, sitting up, head raised in surprise. The courtroom was silent. Warlock ended the silence.

'It seems odd to me you never told the police, for whom you are a witness, that although the *Isle of Arran* left Barry on June 2nd, *she had returned on June 4th*, with engine trouble. It seems curious to me you never explained that there were several days when you were free to leave the ship while repairs were carried out. It seems strange to me you never volunteered the information that the final date for leaving the dock was June 12th, so that you were still in the Cardiff area before and after the date on which Donna Stark died. And I see from the consternation on the face of my learned friend that he considers it strange also.'

Warlock paused, raised his eyebrows and sneered. 'Of course, on the other hand, *you* may see nothing strange in it at all.'

* * *

On his way out of the courthouse Crow managed to snatch a few words with Dewi Jones again.

'He flayed him,' he said.

'Jack Scales?'

Crow nodded.

'Didn't you carry out a check on the sailings from the docks?' Crow asked.

Jones shrugged unhappily.

'It was done, but I suppose it wasn't done thoroughly enough. I mean, we had Evans's confession, we learned the bloody freighter left when Scales said it did and now you say Warlock has proved Scales left something out, if he didn't actually lie . . .'

'It's worse than that,' Crow said calmly. 'Warlock questioned Scales about Donna Stark. He sowed the seeds of doubt by suggesting that Scales was in love with her and might have had motive enough to want to stop her returning to her husband. And now he's shown Scales to be a liar. You see the points? First, Scales maybe had a motive for lying: second, he did lie, by omission, at least and third, if he lied on this, with motive, is any of his testimony to be regarded as trustworthy?'

Jones was silent for a moment.

'Aye, I know . . .You warned us. You told us to go slow. But the Chief Super—'

'There's Skene to come yet. I want to see how Warlock handles him. He's discredited, to a large extent, two of your witnesses already. I'm beginning to think our Mr Evans is a clever fellow, and Warlock is the support he needs.'

'It don't follow—'

'It's what our friends in the States call 'double jeopardy',' Crow said grimly.

* * *

Much of the effusive garrulity that Jones and Crow had seen in Teddy Skene, the enquiry agent, was not apparent in the courtroom. The man seemed appreciative of the solemnity and dignity of the occasion and was content to restrain himself. Crow felt that Skene was once again playing a part, nevertheless: it was possible he was being careful in the face of the obvious cynicism of Jason Warlock, but it was more likely that he was displaying the traits that Crow had already observed in him – the capacity to be what his audience wanted him to be.

Warlock wanted answers and he got them, controlled, precise, carefully constructed answers that dispensed with verbiage and concentrated on the issue in hand.

'I understand you were born in the Rhondda?' Warlock asked.

'That's right. Treherbert.'

'And you now work in Cardiff.'

'That's so. My job as an enquiry agent takes me further afield, of course.'

'You ever go abroad?'

Skene hesitated, then shook his head.

'No, for my clients are mainly local, and not moneyed people. I've been abroad, of course, for I was in the Army for a while and spent some time in Cyprus.'

'Of course.' Warlock paused, consulted the notes in front of him, and Skene stood very still, his eyes fixed on Warlock, a placid expression on his face as he awaited continuation of the cross-examination.

'Now tell me,' Warlock continued, 'how long was it since you last saw Jack Scales?'

'Before he brought Mrs Stark to me? Oh, about a year, maybe more.'

'Were you surprised to see him?'

'Yes. But I soon realised he really wanted to go back to sea and knew he could get a berth out of Cardiff or Barry. And the other thing was that he wanted to put Mrs Stark in touch with me.'

'What were his motives in that?'

'He wanted to get rid of her.'

As Warlock's head came up Skene permitted himself the shadow of a smile. He brushed back an errant strand of his thinning brown hair and said, 'I mean, of course, that he no longer wanted her company.'

'And you were to find her husband for her?'

'That was the general idea.'

Warlock nodded thoughtfully.

'You have testified that the task was not an easy one. You stated that Martin Evans had come south, changed his name from Stark to Evans, changed his profession from solicitor to estate agent, buried himself in an area where he could conceivably hope to remain undiscovered for the rest of his life. But you discovered him . . .by chance.'

'I suppose all these things are a matter of luck,' Skene said seriously. 'I had just about reached the end of my enquiries, with no further lines of investigation open to me, when this solicitor I came across in the Cardiff Arms, in Treorchy—'

'Yes, yes, you've told us. What about afterwards? Having been told that Martin Evans was the man you sought, did you go to Pentre to verify the fact?'

'No'

'Why not?'

'Mrs Stark carne to see me next day. I gave her the information, she seemed to accept it, and she could not have paid me for a further day's work anyway. So we called it quits.'

'And you took no further part in the enquiry?'

Skene shook his head.

'None.'

'You did not go to the Rhondda on June 4th, or June 5th, or June 6th, or at any time that week to pursue the enquiries relating to Martin Evans?'

'I did not.'

'And that was the last time you saw Mrs Stark, in Cardiff that day?'

'It was.'

Warlock scratched his lean cheek. He stared hard at Skene but the enquiry agent met his glance unwaveringly.

'I put it to you that you *did* seek out Martin Evans in the Rhondda.'

'No.'

'I put it to you that you were in the Rhondda on June 5th.'

Skene opened his mouth, hesitated, but before he could answer Warlock continued, 'I put it to you that you were in Pentre on June 5th, that you spoke to Mrs Stark during the late afternoon outside Ystrad Rhondda station, that you were still making enquiries relating to Evans on that day.'

'No.' Skene paused after the incisive rebuttal of Warlock's claim. He appeared to be concentrating hard, and after a moment he took a pocketbook out of his jacket and consulted it. Coolly, he said, 'Sorry, may I backtrack? You are right in your information that I was in the Rhondda on June 5th. I was indeed there, but it was on another matter. I did *not* see Mrs Stark, and I was not pursuing the assignment she had given me. It was finished. I was engaged on other business.'

'Your memory is reliable?'

'My notes are.'

'Do you have notes concerning your conduct in Cyprus in 1956?'

The question confused Skene momentarily. It was out of context for him, he was geared to the Stark enquiry and the mention of years gone shook him. Crow noted the speed of his recovery, however, and the way in which his eyes glittered as he replied, 'No, I do not.'

'But you did testify,' Warlock said silkily, 'that you had served in Cyprus. Is there anything more you wish to add about that service record?'

The silence that followed the question grew longer as Skene considered the matter. Warlock made no attempt to badger him as he thought the matter over; it was obvious to Crow that the longer the silence the better it suited Warlock and the more damaging it was for Skene and the prosecution. At last Skene licked his lips, and leaned forward. He said something in a low voice.

Warlock snapped at him.

'You'll have to speak more clearly!'

'I said I was subjected to a court martial.'

'The result?'

'I was cleared.'

Warlock sneered.

'On a technicality, I understand.'

Skene made no reply. Warlock raised the paper he held in his hand.

'I have a record here, which comprises a summary of the findings of the court. You were given a dishonourable discharge after serving a period in a military prison for complicity in a smuggling operation involving the theft of Army trucks and equipment. The major charge of involvement in the sale of drugs purloined from Army stores was not proceeded with after a witness who could have testified to your involvement suffered an accident while sea-bathing. Is that correct?'

Skene made no reply. His earlier impassiveness had turned to controlled indifference: he was not on trial here. Warlock thought otherwise.

'An interesting document, this record. And your discharge papers. . .the sum total of the comments suggests the court martial was rather less than satisfied about certain aspects of your testimony. To put it plainly, the court was of the opinion you were lying in your testimony given before them.'

Weir, counsel for the prosecution, rose in protest.

'Whatever a court martial may have thought does not amount to proof — and even if it did, such proof would apply to a charge of perjury as before that court martial, not before this court. I must protest, for my learned friend is dealing in matters that are irrelevant to this present hearing!'

'*Irrelevant?*' Warlock raised an amazed eyebrow. 'Is it irrelevant here that the prosecution seeks to use, as a witness to truth, a man who has the sort of record Skene can show? Theft, drug-smuggling, perjury—'

Weir was still protesting vigorously at Warlock's tactics in introducing as fact, matters unproved in law as Crow left. But that, Crow thought to himself, was no unusual state of affairs for Jason Warlock.

* * *

'There are many examples of irrational thinking and behaviour in the application of justice,' the professor said. 'The law states that a man is responsible when he has to answer for his own actions, but such responsibility has been attributed, illogically and yet with a curious absolute logic, to things, animals and even corpses. According to Pausanias in the fourth century BC a statue was condemned to death by drowning in the sea because its fall had caused a man's death. In 1773 the judges of Lorraine enjoined the mice infesting the region to withdraw in three days because their presence had damaged the crops. Exodus itself states : "*If an ox gore a man or a woman that they die, then the ox shall surely be stoned and his flesh shall not be eaten*". Pausanias, again, speaks of the Court of the Prytaneum where they try the axe, and sometimes acquit it, of killing the man . . .'

Crow glanced at his watch. It was too late to attempt to leave the conference now and attend the session in the magistrates court. He was not particularly interested in the lecture, concerned as it was with *'Collaboration between Doctors and Jurists — the Basis of a New Penal Justice'*, but it did give him the chance to sit and think.

While he had been watching the conduct of Warlock's defence he had also been observing Martin Evans, and Crow continued to be struck by the air of resigned submissiveness he affected. It puzzled Crow; if Evans was being clever he was masking it well, for capitulation still seemed to be his watchword. He had even shown a certain irritation at some points where Warlock had been attacking the witnesses and seeking to discredit their testimony.

And Warlock had done a pretty good job of that, Crow thought grimly.

'. . . in the Italian School of Criminology,' the professor was droning on, 'it is suggested a man cannot be held morally responsible since his behaviour is the result of many factors operating independently on his own will; he must however be considered socially responsible when he attacks the organisation of the community, the safety or the *mores* of its members. Not criminal responsibility, but social defence.'

It would be Dai Davies, the fish-and-chip merchant, who would be facing Warlock today.

Crow wondered what Warlock would do to Davies. He remembered his own interview with the fish-and-chip merchant, his own scepticism at the argument that Davies had recognized a brooch worn by the dead woman when he had seen it, and her, only once, about ten in the evening as it was getting dark. Ten in the evening on Tuesday, June 6th . . .

On a sudden impulse, Crow fished in his pocket for his diary even though he had checked it before. Sure enough, Tuesday had been the 6th, and it fitted with the fish-fryer's story.

But there was something there that bothered Crow; he wondered whether it would have bothered Warlock also . . .

The man next to Crow rose to his feet suddenly and said something in a loud voice. Startled, Crow turned to stare at him and then realised that the professor had finished his talk and questions were to be asked. The man on Crow's right had been the first questioner. The professor was starting to answer.

'A good point, a good point. What indeed is the rationale behind the law? If the idea is to protect young girls, the offence is already covered by that of unlawful sexual intercourse. Can there be eugenic reasons for the abhorrence with which the offence is treated? Dr Allen has shown in his *Textbook of Psychosexual Disorders* that no studies have satisfactorily been made of the offspring of such unions — they do not occur with sufficient frequency. Certainly, it is not abnormal among animals, it was practised by the Aztecs and by Cambyses of Persia. The modern view—'

'One moment, Professor,' the man beside Crow insisted. 'We have been discussing an offence that was cognizable by ecclesiastical courts until 1908 except for a period during 1650 until 1660, and it now seems ridiculous that the feeble coercion of the spiritual court should have been replaced by the harshness of the temporal criminal court.'

Crow began to rise; he had no idea what they were talking about and it was time he left to see the Chief Constable. The professor at the rostrum stared at him in brief irritation, then ignored him as he went on,

'Exactly my point, my dear sir. The modern view, as I was about to say, is still dominated by the Levitical injunction and the rigorous hostility of the Judaic-Christian ethic. This must be the basis of the taboo, it is certainly based more upon deeply seated psychological and religious grounds than on a knowledge of eugenics. But,' he continued, his voice booming to the back of the hall as Crow slipped quietly out, 'think of the people concerned. For them, in this modern world, must life be a tragedy, must love be a crime . . .?'

* * *

The Chief Constable and the Chief Superintendent were both waiting in the broad, oak-panelled office in the County buildings near the court. The Chief Superintendent stood by the window; he was in a bad temper, but Crow was not prepared to pull any punches in this interview simply to save the Chief Superintendent's feelings.

The Chief Constable was more controlled but he was less closely concerned, obviously; it was not on his desk that the buck would lie. He was worried, nevertheless. He waved Crow to a chair. Crow perched himself on the edge of the brown leather seat and placed his hands on his knees. He felt vaguely annoyed, and the feeling of annoyance disturbed him for he wanted to remain cool in this matter.

The fact was, of course, he had not wanted his original role to be merely advisory in the first instance; had it been a normal role he would have had more control over decisions and the present situation would not have arisen.

He gained no satisfaction from the fact things were not going well; it was a reflection upon all police cases if this one failed.

"This man Warlock is no fool,' said the Chief Constable, massively stating the obvious.

'Did he give Mr Davies a rough time this morning?' Crow asked. 'I wasn't in court.'

'He gave him a rough time,' the Chief Constable said, intoning the words like a requiem. 'The matter of dates came up, and where Davies had been so positive about Tuesday the 6th of June when he gave evidence to us, he is less than positive now. Warlock made him admit that he could have been mistaken. He stuck to the date under re-examination by Weir, of course, and that saved the situation, but Warlock had certainly made him sweat. I must confess I don't quite see why Warlock is going to all this trouble, but he's making a mess of our witnesses nevertheless, casting doubt on their veracity—'

'That's the whole point,' Crow said quietly. 'He's going to make a submission of no case to answer.'

The Chief Superintendent humphed and walked across the room to take a seat. The Chief Constable scowled thoughtfully.

'The magistrates won't accept that plea.'

Crow agreed.

'I don't think they will, but the reason why Warlock is pressing now is that he wants all the evidence from these witnesses down on record. He's well aware this case is hastily presented, far from complete—'

'I can't say that I—' the Chief Superintendent began, but the Chief Constable silenced him with a quick gesture.

'As I was saying,' Crow continued in a steely voice, 'this case came to prosecution before enough work had been done on it. Warlock is sensitive and long experienced; he guessed how the wind blew. So he's roasted each witness and roasted them well. He took James Klein and showed him up to be a man with a shady background who could even have ended up in prison himself; he picked Jack Scales to pieces by emphasising that the man had been less than truthful in his statements to the police — who, incidentally, were shown up as not having done their homework properly; and he went to town afterwards on this man Skene. I interviewed Skene with Inspector Jones and thought him a slippery customer, outwardly direct, if garrulous, but a man to be watched. Warlock seized him, shook him, and showed him to be a man with a record of possible perjury, and dishonesty. Now what does all this mean?'

'You tell us,' the Chief Constable said coldly.

'It means that the prosecution have brought forward as witnesses to testify against Martin Evans a collection of people who, between them, have very few honest bones in their bodies. The prosecution can produce no witnesses as to the murder, no connection between Evans and the dead woman other than proximity to the pit head and the shaft and the office — and marital ties of some age. And if what you say about Mr Davies is correct, the prosecution cannot even fix the date when Davies saw her in Pentre — fix it with any exactitude, anyway.'

'So what do you suggest we do?' the Chief Superintendent said grumpily.

'It's not too late even now," Crow said. 'Pull out all the stops. To start with, check whether Skene actually did come to the valley during that period as Warlock suggested. Warlock may have information we don't. Or he may have been bluffing. Check on Scales's movements after the *Isle of Arran* returned with her damaged engines. Check all the little things you didn't check before. And do it fast. Warlock's done damage; if this case reaches the Crown Court we need to plug the gaps.'

'It'll reach the Crown Court all right,' the Chief Superintendent said angrily. 'If you don't mind me saying so I think we are overreacting. This man Warlock has chased these witnesses around the courtroom a bit but he hasn't got them to change their stories, has he?'

Crow stared at the Chief Superintendent aware that the turn of events rankled with him, aware he was very much on the defensive. But it was too late in the day to be gentle with him.

'I think I'd better spell it out for you.' Crow spoke quietly, his deep-set eyes fixed on the Chief Superintendent. 'Your witnesses have not let you down, yet. But they will. Warlock has shown gaps, he's inviting us to plug them. If we don't, he'll tear their testimony wide open in the Crown Court. If we do, and if the stories given by the witnesses in the Crown Court differ much in an attempt to plug the gaps, he'll tear us apart and accuse the prosecution of tampering with the evidence. What he's done in court so far is to cast doubts on the witnesses — he'll do a damn sight more later. If the magistrates say there is a case to answer, and my guess is that they will, you can look out for fireworks in the Crown Court.'

'But I don't see—' began the Chief Superintendent.

'The facts are simple,' Crow interrupted him firmly. 'Dai Davies is doubtful about dates; Skene may still have been involved with the case *after* he says he was; Scales could still have been around when Mrs Stark died, and he certainly lied to you about his departure; we still need to know how deeply Klein is concerned and whether he really was on a business trip when she died. But above all, there's Evans's confession.'

The Chief Superintendent shook his head.

'We've got him there,' he insisted. 'That's one thing that will still stand up.'

'It's never stood up with me,' Crow said quietly.

Both men stared at him. Crow sat still and contemplated his shoes. After a charged silence, it was the Chief Constable who found his tongue first.

'But you were there when he confessed!'

'That's why I've been uneasy about it all along.'

The Chief Superintendent snorted derisively.

'Aw, come on! I've read that statement. It's clear and precise. Martin Evans takes the whole thing on himself and supplies motive, opportunity and act. It's the best bit of evidence I've ever seen in such a case, and it was given in front of two senior officers, written down, signed . . . and *now* you say you have doubts about it. For crying out loud—'

'I'd better make myself clear, Chief Superintendent. You will recall I advised against proceeding immediately with the prosecution. This was one of the reasons. As you so rightly say, I was there when Evans was questioned. The statement is clear, as you say. But I've never been happy about the circumstances in which it was given.'

The Chief Constable hitched himself forward in his chair, linked his fingers together anxiously and frowned at Crow.

'Are you now telling us that Warlock will have grounds for upsetting the confession? Dammit, man—'

'Let me finish,' Crow interrupted quietly. 'I don't think there are grounds as such, provided Evans is still going along with what he said. It's just that I'm curious, and always have been curious about that interview we conducted. You see, it went like this. When we arrived to question Evans he was in a state of shock: he was facing the truth, the fact of his wife's death. Oh, I know he was aware that she was dead, but it was as though he had thrust it away from him, hoping his link with her could never be discovered. But now it had, and he was unwilling to accept it immediately.'

'Was he in that state when he gave his confession?' the Chief Constable asked anxiously.

Crow shook his head.

'That was only the first stage. Inspector Jones asked him a few questions and he gradually snapped out of his shock, his reluctance disappeared, and he became more alert. More, he became defensive, in a very controlled way. He admitted nothing — *but he asked us what we knew.*'

The Chief Constable raised his eyebrows. The inflection and emphasis Crow used meant nothing to him and he showed his puzzlement openly. Crow smiled grimly.

'It's common enough as a manoeuvre. He simply did not want to admit to anything he need not; he needed to discover what we knew before he made a statement.'

'But he *confessed*,' the Chief Superintendent said angrily.

'Not immediately,' Crow replied, 'He got us to paint the picture. He denied knowledge of the murder in the first instance and then Jones—'

Crow paused, hesitated over making it seem as though Jones had gone too quickly, too soon, and amended the statement. 'And then we put our case to him, we told him how we saw it all add up, we named names . . . And Evans changed again, in demeanour.'

'How do you mean?' The Chief Constable was watching Crow carefully, and with more respect now. He had realised the manner in which Crow was to some extent covering for Inspector Jones's precipitate behaviour in questioning Evans, and much of his earlier bluster was disappearing.

'You say he was shocked first, then defensive — ,

'He had changed once more. He was nervous again, And after we underlined the motive for murder, the fact of the destruction of his business through gossip well, he lapsed into deep thought after that and it was as though we weren't there. It was at that point, I believe, that *decisions were reached* by Martin Evans. And once he reached them, he confessed to the murder of his wife.'

There was a brief silence where all digested the meaning behind his words.

'All right,' the Chief Superintendent said. 'So he decided, so he confessed. Quick and clean.'

The Chief Constable was more perceptive, or less involved in terms of pride. He nodded, still staring at Crow. He was beginning to understand.

'You've been worried ever since, the longer you think about it.'

'That's right,' Crow said. 'something happened to Martin Evans during the course of the interview and at that point he reached a decision. He had never intended confessing but he'd been anxious and scared. He came to himself, he got out of us just what we knew, and then he sank into a deep consideration as to what he should do about it all. And his decision —'

'Was a *confession*!' the Chief Superintendent almost shouted. 'Hell, man, you know how it is. Anxiety, remorse—'

'No.' Crow's voice was incisive. 'Shock, anxiety, then a controlled leading of us in a defensive pattern, then consideration, then confession. It's not a normal pattern, damn it, you must see that! It's been bothering me ever since we arrested him. The confession wasn't . . . natural I tell you, I was at a lecture recently and it was only then the thing crystallized for me. The lecturer was talking about body temperature, the constants for the corpse. That was it, you see, when a man's dead you can apply constants — temperature, warmth of the room, body, environment —

but when a man's *alive* what are the constants? None, or few, because men react differently to their surroundings and their environment. And that's what we don't know. That's what we need to know. We need to discover what Evans was reacting to when he confessed!'

'He was reacting to you and Inspector Jones and his guilt and the fact of his wife's death and the long wait until the body was discovered and the massive blow to his hopes she'd never be discovered. . .Hell—' the Chief Superintendent waved an angry arm, 'the list is endless.'

'It could be all of those,' Crow said quietly. 'But it could be more too. Something we don't know about; something we *should* know about.'

'And that,' the Chief Constable added, 'is why you didn't want us to press on so quickly with the prosecution.'

Crow inclined his head. The point was made; he was not going to rub it in.

'At that time I wasn't able to explain things so positively, even to myself. Then it was just a feeling something was wrong; now it's a conviction.' He rubbed his right hand over his bony left wrist in a gesture of self-doubt. He hesitated before speaking. 'I think Evans is still hiding something.'

'You'll tell us you think he's not guilty next,' the Chief Superintendent grumbled.

'No,' Crow said slowly. 'There's guilt in the man. It was in his face when we first walked into his office. He was full of guilt about the death of Donna Stark. I'm sure of that, but there's something else, something we don't yet know . . .'

'I think you've made the point,' the Chief Constable said. 'The case is now adjourned for the weekend after tomorrow. I shouldn't think Warlock will call witnesses for the defence. They'll be held in reserve. His submission of no case won't be until next Tuesday, I should think, when we've finished our case. After that it's got to go to the Crown Court—'

'We'll need to act quickly,' Crow said. 'I propose I commence an immediate and full investigation into Evans's background and history. You'll clear it with Commander Gray?'

The Chief Constable nodded. He pulled towards him the file on Martin Evans, read it for a few minutes and then nodded again. He looked up at Crow; they were of one mind now.

'You'll have to get out to Canada as quickly as possible,'

'Canada?' the Chief Superintendent said in stupefaction. 'What the hell do we expect to get from there?'

Crow stood up and reached for the file on the Chief Constable's desk.

'With luck, a few answers—and maybe the truth.'

CHAPTER 6

The menu was in French and English. As they lunched on a pedigreed lobster in the century-old sea-food bar Crow commented upon the menu to his host. George Grattan smiled and wiped his mouth with his napkin.

'Been eating here in English for years, before seventy French CBC employees marched in and demanded their orders got taken in French. Changed since then.'

'I gather the same kind of problems have arisen in Wales of recent years,' Crow said,

'That so? Minorities, hey? Tell you, time was, the most important minority around here was the millionaires — forty-two of them lived within a mile of this spot. But Montreal is changing, I tell you. Sure, the Old Quarter is still a maze of cobbled streets, sailors' taverns and Louis Quinze churches you can still get home-cured tobacco and pigeon pies in Bonsecours Market; Sherbrooke Street is still elegant with its elms and grey stone mansions, but most of them are now converted to luxury shops and the rich have fled up Mount Royal.'

'You haven't.'

George Grattan chuckled, cracked his lobster claw and wiped his fingers. He was a big man in a wrinkled grey suit. He sat squarely and comfortably in his chair, solid, dependable, reliable as a favourite hound. He looked like one in fact, Crow had decided, with his sad eyes that would never betray surprise or accept doubt, his dewlaps around his chin and his long, heavy face.

But he had the persistence of a hound too, once he had caught sight of his quarry: when Crow had arrived at the office for his appointment Grattan had simply swept him out again, taken him for a swift tour through the Old Quarter and then treated him to an expensive lunch.

'Looks like you need fattenin',' he had said amiably, brooking no protest. Crow had given in.

Grattan chuckled again, a rich sound thick as gravy, as he extracted the last morsels of meat from the claw.

'There's rich, and rich,' he said. 'I'm sixty now and sure, I could retire, I got enough money behind me, the business has really boomed these last ten years. It's changed Montreal to a concrete and glass jungle but that's not my affair. I build what I get paid to build. But I like to keep an office down this part of town, if only for access to the Old Quarter.'

His sad eyes grew reflective.

'But times sure is changing. Lot different from the time when we got started.'

'That's really what I'd like to hear about,' Crow said. 'About the old times, when you started in business with Alan Stark.'

'Alan? I thought it was Martin you were interested in. Fine lad, Martin. I was sorry to see him leave. He never kept in touch, neither, not after the first couple of years"

'I'd like to hear about the Alan Stark you knew, first, by way of background,' Crow said.

Grattan nodded, beckoned to the waiter and ordered coffee. It was served almost immediately and Grattan took his black.

'Background, hey?' he said. 'Well, lemme see, what can I tell you? The way things were in 1939? The war? The building boom? You can get all that from books and newspapers, I reckon. It's Alan Stark you want to know about. Okay, he was about six feet tall — unusual for a Welsh miner, I reckon, they're short and dark, ain't that so? Good-looking feller, dark hair, handsome, blue scar on his forehead from a pit accident. But he'd have been wasted in Wales in the mines, you know that? He came to Canada with his wife Jean — pretty kid, she was too, blonde, a bit fluffy, but good-natured and adored Alan — and Martin would be about three years old then, a lively kid. They came to Montreal in '39 with just a few dollars between them. Alan worked all sorts of hours until he got himself a stake, and then he bought a truck, then another, built up a small trucking business until in '43 he was doing well — and he merged with my old man's building firm.'

Grattan sipped his coffee, clucked his tongue in appreciation and looked around him with satisfaction.

'It was a good day for my old man when Alan Stark went in with him. The main thing you got to remember is that a firm can founder unless new blood comes in. Alan Stark was raw as hell, had no business background but in a strange way that helped considerably — he came up with ideas no one else thought of and the business went ahead. It was good. And after Jean died . . . that would be about 1949 . . . he really worked his guts out.'

Grattan glanced covertly at Crow and smiled.

'Course, I don't want to give the impression Alan Stark was all work. He used to play too. Why, when we were across in Vancouver one time, there was this party, she was built like a . . . well, I won't go into that . . . After Jean died, though, a lot of the fun went out of him. He had a woman tucked away for a while, just outside town, but never went too good. And then he got killed.'

'What happened?' Crow asked.

'Car accident,' Grattan said shortly. Ploughed right into a truck. Funny that, in a way . . . he built up a business by trucking and then ended up under the crushed cab of one. Bad business altogether . . .'

'How did Martin take it?'

'Ah well, Martin . . .' Grattan finished his coffee, waited until the waiter had served him and Crow a second time, and then turned back to Crow. 'It was about this time Martin was making his way in the business. Alan Stark had come up the hard, entrepreneurial way with nothing behind him but grit and native intelligence. He wanted Martin to start different. They had a talk when Martin left school and he got him fixed up at law school. Once he qualified Martin came into the firm all right, but as a qualified lawyer, and he worked to build up a sound legal section so we didn't need to rely on outside firms. Things had gone well and the legal department was solid when Alan died.'

'That was in . . .?'

'Oh, hell, when was it . . . 1957 or 1958? As I recall Martin was about twenty-two, anyway it happened near to his birthday. But you asked how he took it, well, he took it bad.'

'Was he close to his father?'

Grattan nodded emphatically.

'Pretty close. Bit of an odd character really; solid on principle. I mean, he was a lawyer, and his old man had been a miner, a trucker and at the end a businessman but Martin took something from his mother too, a sort of quiet, almost religious outlook on life. A good churchgoer, you know. Small Methodist place, they went to, him and his mother, till she died. 'Course, she'd have been chapel-going in Wales. They're strong on that there, huh?'

'There's a chapel near every bus stop in the Rhondda,' Crow said. 'And a pub.'

Grattan chuckled and finished his coffee.

'Good marketing techniques there, I reckon. Get off the bus, take your choice! Anyway, like I said, Martin was pretty cut up after his father died. I was executor to Alan's will and Martin took over the handling of it all. And that's really how he came to cut loose from the firm, I guess.'

'How do you mean?'

Grattan snapped his fingers for the bill.

'Well, it was like this. Martin wasn't too happy, I reckon, continuing to work with the firm after Alan died. They was pretty close, as I said, particularly after Martin's mother died. Well, there he was, legal adviser to the company, his father just dead, and I guess he felt footloose, unsettled. The will gave him the push or the excuse he needed. He left us.'

'What in the will gave him the push?'

Grattan took the bill from the waiter, scrutinized it, then signed it and handed it back. The waiter bowed obsequiously and moved away. Grattan took a toothpick from the glass in front of him and began to pick at his front teeth.

'You got to remember,' he said, 'over the years Jean and Alan Stark never forgot their homeland. They were typically Welsh, I understand, in that they kept their accents — though Martin had an accent that was half Welsh and half Montreal, if you know what I mean — and they kept their affection for Wales. I hear they're all like that, the Welsh — think their country's really special and all that. Anyway, the fact is Alan talked about the Rhon. . .the Rhond. . .'

'The Rhondda.'

'Rontha, yeah, that's it,' Grattan said with satisfaction, and inspected a piece of lobster meat on his toothpick. 'He talked about it a great deal, and when he'd had a few whiskies he'd get real homesick, you know? Well, inevitably, I guess, it had its effect upon young Martin. And after his father died, the will was read and there was a clause in it that gave Martin the incentive, the push he needed. It was a legacy, payable to a friend of the family.'

'What friend?'

Grattan shook his head regretfully.

'You got me there, too long ago for me to remember, but you could always check through probate, of course. But as far as I can make out, it was this way. Alan Stark grew up in the Rhondda and married a local girl, Jean. Both he and Jean were pretty thick with another couple who must have got married the same time and they remained friends right up until the time Alan Stark brought his wife and kiddie to Canada. After that, I don't know the story exactly, but I guess both these friends must have got killed or something, because there was no mention of them in the will. The legacy was to their daughter, and that was Martin's reason for leaving us here in Montreal.'

'You mean he decided to pay the legacy to this girl in person?' Crow asked.

'That's about the way it was. You got to remember, the will named this girl and Martin had to trace her. He made enquiries by letter first of all but learned, far as I recall, that this girl wasn't living in the valley any more. So he decided he'd go across there and find her.'

'In Wales?'

'Not so. England, far as I could learn.' Grattan frowned and tossed his toothpick aside. 'The girl had left the valley, was working somewhere in London. Martin wrote me about it. Told me how he had some difficulty tracing her but finally made it. Paid her the legacy soon as he found her. Same letter he told me he was pulling out of the firm here in Montreal. Left it to me to fix a price for his shares. There was no argument about it. So I transmitted the money to him about six months later. Thought it would come in as a useful windfall at that time — along with the present I sent.'

'Present?'

Grattan scratched at his dewlap.

'Yeah. Wedding Present.'

There was a short silence. At last Crow asked quietly 'You mean Martin Stark *married* this girl?'

George Grattan was no fool; he caught the inflection and stared at John Crow.

'You didn't get around to telling me yet,' he said wryly, 'just what all this questioning is in aid of. I know it's an investigation of some sort but you ain't been very helpful. Martin's in trouble, I know that, but—'

'He's charged with the murder of his wife,' Crow said. Grattan's face became fixed with astonishment and he blinked twice, as though trying to brush Crow and what he was saying from his consciousness.

'He *murdered* the girl?'

Crow frowned; he was puzzled. Things weren't fitting quite into place.

'This friend of the family — are you sure Martin Stark married her?'

'He was all set to. Told me he'd found her, paid her the legacy, got friendly, fell in love, and they was getting married. But *murder*!'

'When was it he would have married her?' Crow asked sharply.

'Hell, within the year of meeting her, I guess. I mean, it was in '58 he went over there, he wrote a bit later to say he'd met her, then within a couple of months it was a letter to say they was getting married and he was pulling out of Montreal and the business.'

'You don't remember her name?' Crow said. 'Would it be Donna?'

Grattan shook his head immediately.

'Surely not. This girl, she had a Welsh name.'

'And Martin Stark married her in 1958 or 1959. The woman he is charged with murdering is a woman he married in 1964.'

'He was married twice? I didn't know about that. So what happened to the first one? The one he paid the legacy to?'

'That's precisely what we have to find out,' Crow said.

* * *

A transatlantic call to Inspector Dewi Jones was necessary to get the wheels in motion immediately for the checks to be carried out at registry offices. George Grattan had been unable to help on the question of location, though he thought the first marriage had been celebrated in London. Crow relayed his instructions to Jones and learned in addition that the Chief Superintendent was personally supervising the checks on the stories of the other witnesses.

'And how did you get on with our friend Warlock?' Crow asked.

Jones's voice sounded brittle and unfamiliar over the crackling line but its tone was plain enough.

'He gave me a rough time. And at the end of it all he asked for the magistrates to declare there was no case for Martin Evans to answer.'

'What did they say to that?'

'Predictably, they disagreed with him, but they took their time considering it. And one of them had a word with the Chief Constable later — old boys' network and all that. He didn't like the witnesses we'd served up and thought the whole thing a bit fishy.'

'Warlock will make it smell fishier in the Crown Court hearing. When's it scheduled for?'

'Don't know yet. But Warlock's made a plea for a swift hearing in view of his submission that the charges against his client have no foundation in fact. The magistrates were impressed. I think there's every chance of an early hearing so we'll have to get our skates on.'

'I'll be back in two days,' Crow promised.

* * *

Dewi Jones met him at Heathrow on his return and drove with him to Tonypandy after the flight to Cardiff. Crow gave him the documents he had brought back with him.

'Last will and testament of Alan Stark,' Crow said. 'There's the clause mentioning the legacy payable to the girl.'

Jones read it silently, then nodded.

'Ahuh. Well, I've got papers too — marriage certificate of Stark and the girl. Registry office in Paddington, October, 1959.'

'On his "marriage" to Donna, did Martin state he'd been married before, and divorced?'

'He did not. Described himself as a bachelor when he married Donna Stark; there's no evidence of a divorce from his first wife, so he lied, and was therefore a bigamist when he walked down the aisle with Donna. But there's another thing I want to show you. Divorce papers.'

'But you said—'

'Not Martin Stark's — divorce papers for Annie and Fred Williams.'

'Who the hell are they !' Crow asked in exasperation.

'A couple who were friendly with the Starks before the emigration to Canada. Fred Williams was a miner during the war, killed in a roof collapse in 1945. But he divorced Annie in 1942. . .the grounds were her adultery with an American soldier. There was a lot of it about at that time! Anyway, she went back to the States with the soldier in question. The daughter of her marriage to Fred stayed behind though, with Fred. Ceinwen, her name was. She stayed with her father until he was killed in the pit and then she was brought up by her grandmother, on Annie's side. The grandmother is dead now too, a little while back. She was called Sarah Parry.'

'So the woman called Ceinwen Williams is our mystery girl,' Crow said. 'She was the daughter of Alan Stark's friend; she was the one he mentioned in his will;

she was the one Martin Stark met, paid the legacy to, and then married. But never got divorced from, before he married again. But this name, Ceinwen Williams, it's familiar . . .'

'It's the woman who works in the office, for Martin Evans. Ceinwen Williams. He's been employing as an assistant the wife he never got divorced from.'

* * *

She sat in her chair in the sitting-room, quietly, hands clasped in her lap, eyes downcast. She was a reserved person, Crow could see that, not a woman who would be likely to send flames of desire leaping in a man, but a woman who would make a good wife. Like his own wife Martha, for instance. Quiet, dependable, aware of his needs. But hardly a *femme fatale*, and hardly the kind of woman Crow would expect to find in this curious, triangular relationship.

'Did you know Martin was a bigamist?' Crow asked her, and her eyes flickered sadly up to his, glanced towards the silent Dewi Jones, and then looked down again. She shook her head.

'But you must have suspected it. I mean, did he never talk about the years he spent in Newcastle?'

Again she shook her head. Crow looked at Jones, frowning. They were getting nowhere with Ceinwen Williams; she was frightened, but she was loyal too. And she was prepared to say nothing that might incriminate Martin. Crow sensed that there was a strong bond of affection, if not love, between her and her employer and he was puzzled by it, and by the situation. He tried again.

'We've come here today, Miss Williams, to try to piece together exactly what has happened, and how Donna Stark came to die. You say you did not know Martin had "married" again. But the story we have so far is this. You were brought up by your grandmother after your father died and your mother had gone to the States.'

Ceinwen Williams nodded.

'Gran Parry,' she said in a nervous whisper.

'When you were eighteen you went to live in London with a cousin, and you worked there as a typist for a few years. Then, when you were twenty or thereabouts, Martin Stark appeared. He told you a legacy had been left to you by his father; he paid you the money; he courted you, and you got married in October 1959.'

Again she nodded, without looking up.

'So what went wrong?' Crow asked.

She made no reply. Crow persisted.

'I must ask you, Miss Williams. You did not live with Martin long. You came back here to the Rhondda and returned to live with Mrs Parry again. Why did you do that? What happened between you and Martin?'

She shook her head in quiet desperation. 'Things just, well . . . they didn't work out.'

Her voice was quiet but there was an odd inflection that puzzled Crow. She was afraid, he knew that; afraid of the police, of the questions, of the dredging up of the past, maybe even of Crow's appearance. But there was another fear; it was the one he wanted to know about.

'All right. Things didn't work out. You quarrelled?'

'It was . . . yes, all right, something like that.'

'You came to the Rhondda, and Martin left London, went to Newcastle. Why go to the north-east?'

'To escape, I suppose.'

'Escape from what?'

She made no reply and Crow could only guess that she meant escape from the wreckage of his marriage.

'All right. He left London, you parted, he qualified as an English solicitor in the north-east, he joined a firm, he met a woman called Donna — and he married her. Tell me this, why did he not get a divorce first? Did you oppose it?'

Ceinwen Williams looked up quickly, a flash of anger illuminating her eyes for the first time and bringing life to her face.

'I never did that. I never knew he married again. And if he had told me, if he had asked for a divorce, I would never have opposed it!'

'He never asked but just went ahead and remarried?'

The anger still blazed in her face. She opened her mouth to speak but a shadow touched her eyes, the anger faded, the anxiety and the fear came over her again and she made no reply. Dumbly, she shook her head.

In a gentle tone, Crow said, 'You must be reasonable, help me to see how things were. You know the case against Martin. I want to know how everything fits together, for there are some things about his confession that puzzle me. Now tell me: you never heard from Martin after he went to Newcastle?'

'He . . . he wrote a few times. We corresponded.'

'But he never told you he remarried?'

'No.'

'Nor about having to leave his firm?'

She hesitated, then shook her head.

'No. He just appeared here in Treherbert one day. He told me he had decided to come to live in the Rhondda, had bought up Morgan and Enoch the estate agents, was going to live and work there in Pentre. He . . . he asked me to go to work with him.'

Crow stared at her, puzzled.

'Just that? To work for him?'

'Yes.'

'But you and he were still legally married! Why did he not suggest you tried again, tried to make a go of your marriage?'

Her face was stiff, her hands twisting, one inside the other. She tried to speak, failed, at last found her voice, but her tone was strangled.

'It . . . it wasn't like that. I was to work for him.'

Crow glanced at Dewi Jones in something close to despair. He was lost; incapable of understanding these people and not certain whether it was their native Welsh closeness and distrust of outsiders that made it impossible or whether it was simply that Ceinwen Williams had nothing to say or refused to speak out of fear. But fear of what?

'Did you see Donna Stark when she came?'

'No. I never knew about her . . . until you came that day, and arrested Martin. He . . . he said nothing.'

'You mean he never mentioned her visit?' Crow was incredulous. 'She must have written to him at his office. Did you not know about that? Or the blackmail letter?'

Her eyes flashed again.

'I know nothing of a blackmail letter, but she was an evil woman, I am certain of that, plaguing Martin in that way, demanding money from him, threatening to . . .'

She fell silent. Crow waited. At last he leaned forward, frowning.

'Threatening to do what?'

She shook her head again, and exasperated, Crow said, 'It's all too much to believe. You *must* have known about her. You were close to Martin, you worked together here all these years, you had been man and wife, and yet he never told you about. . ..' Crow paused, watching the agony mount in her quiet face.

'He . . . he was *protecting* you, Ceinwen. Was that it?'

But protecting her from what?

* * *

Crow and Dewi Jones made their way back to the car. They had parked it in a side street because as Jones had explained it never did to drive right up to the door; the neighbours would be out on the street doorsteps waiting for the police to come out again and it could be an uncomfortable experience for a woman like Ceinwen Williams to be the centre of such attention. He had suggested it would be better if they walked a few streets from the car to interview her.

When they reached the car Crow hesitated, looked about him at the bright blue sky and the hills, and demurred at returning to headquarters in Tonypandy. He suggested walking up on to the hillside, so Dewi Jones led the way into the first bend of the Rhigos, up past the hospital, the big Welshman breathing hard as they climbed, the Englishman less short of breath and longer in the leg. They reached the hairpin bend and crossed it, then found a seat where they could look down into the beginnings of the valley, and up towards Blaencwm and the craggy solid shoulders of the mountain beyond. For perhaps the first time Crow felt the sense of freedom the mountains could bring; till now he had thought of the Rhondda as a narrow, shut-in place with narrow, shut-in people. But up here, above the slag heaps and the pits and away from the dingy streets, a man could breathe and feel good and unfettered.

Perhaps this was why Martin had come to the valley when his 'marriage' with Donna had broken down.

'I don't understand it,' he murmured.

'What's that, sir?'

Crow smiled, snapped off a blade of grass and began to chew it. He watched some sheep amble across the road, white dots high against the grey surface of the road, the green-grey surface of the mountain.

'It just doesn't make sense. Martin marries Ceinwen but within months leaves for Newcastle and she comes here. But later, when his "marriage" to Donna breaks down for reasons we know about, it's to Ceinwen he returns. But not as man and wife — as employer and employee. It doesn't make sense.'

'I agree.'

'And then again, he didn't tell her about Donna even though he wrote to her. Why not? His marriage to Ceinwen had broken down, why didn't he get a divorce? I just don't understand it, and when Donna came down here to the valley to screw some money out of him, either with that blackmail letter first which Ceinwen says she knew nothing of, or by a face-to-face meeting, what he does is to kill her. But why? Was it to protect himself? I can't see that, because he's doing little to protect himself now with that bloody confession. To protect Ceinwen? She seems to think so even if she's not saying so. But why the hell did he need to protect her—he was the bigamist, not she. Ceinwen Williams was clear; he was the one in trouble. The gossip would have been about him, she'd been just an innocent victim, she'd just have had the sympathy. *What an awful man to marry. . .*'

Crow glanced quickly at Jones, annoyed with himself that he had mimicked a Welsh accent in illustrating the gossip that would have gone on. Jones seemed not to have noticed, but he did not speak, and Crow was sensitive enough to remain quiet for a while, to let the remark and the mimicry fade away into insignificance.

'The answer's important, I'm sure of it,' he said at last. 'What was this Mrs Parry like. . .you know, the grandmother?'

Dewi Jones shrugged.

'I've asked around. A bit of a tartar, I think. She played hell with her daughter Annie when she pushed off with that Yank during the war, but she was quick enough to look after Ceinwen. And give her a home again when she returned from London, after her broken marriage with Martin.'

'Had she ever met Martin?' Crow asked.

'Why do you wonder about that?'

Crow chewed at his grass stem thoughtfully. He pulled it out, inspected it, split and broken. Like Ceinwen's marriage.

'Maybe the grandmother had something to do with breaking it up.'

'If she had, would Ceinwen have returned to live with her?' Jones countered.

Crow shrugged.

'It depends. She'd have been pretty old, maybe she needed someone, maybe she wanted Ceinwen back with her from London and didn't like the idea of the girl marrying . . . But it would take more than that, wouldn't it, much more? Because Ceinwen still loves Martin, I'm damn sure of that. And Martin, well . . .'

'He's protected her in the past,' Jones said.

'Gran Parry, Sarah Parry . . . she's been dead a while now, of course.'

'Couple of years.'

'So any secrets she might have held would have died with her. We're left with Ceinwen and Martin, and they know something, I'm sure, something they won't tell us. Or at least, Martin knows, and somehow . . .'

'Lily Jenkins,' Dewi Jones said thoughtfully.

'I beg your pardon?'

'She might be able to help. Lily Jenkins Secrets.'

Crow threw down the grass stem in a certain exasperation. 'What the hell are you talking about?'

'It's the thing you said about Mrs Parry's secrets dying with her. They might not have done, you see. There's Mrs Jenkins.'

'What about her?'

Dewi Jones wriggled a little uncomfortably.

'You won't know how things are done in the valley, sir. Different from ways outside, over death, I mean. Everyone goes to the church or the chapel, but only the men go in the cars to the cemetery. Stand at the graveside. The women, they all go home, prepare tea for the men when they get back. Then everyone sits around, and drinks tea and eats ham sandwiches — usually paid for out of a whip-around taken in the street — and they talk about the one who's gone, and what he or she was like and so on—'

'A wake,' Crow said.

'More or less. But the whole thing starts earlier than that, really. You see, the undertaker arrives to take the corpse to the chapel of rest, or to arrange flowers and coffin in the front room and all that, but nine times out of ten he'll find half his work done for him. Corpse washed, laid out, clothed, done up nice for viewing.'

'Laid out by whom?'

'By the Lily Jenkinses of this world. Damn, sir, you got to appreciate her kind to understand. They're always old before their time; ancient when they're twenty if you know what I mean. And then they seem to go on for ever. They never marry, they always dress the same way, usually grey or black, they make the best mince pies you ever tasted and they draw a chicken in a flash. Mince pies, drawing Christmas turkeys and laying people out. It's what they live for, their reason for existence.'

The burst of speech was delivered defensively, but Crow's attention was caught and he ignored the flush staining Dewi Jones's features.

'Tell me more.'

'Well, sir,' Jones began, waxing more confident, 'it kind of struck me when you mention secrets, that's what she's called you know, Lily Jenkins Secrets. Thing is, she's a bit different from most other layers-out in the valley. It was always as though she could sniff out the ones likely to die. And she would sit with them, If an old man was sick and pretty old it'd be Lily who'd sit with him, tend him till he finally went. Gave the family some relief, you know? And young people these days, though they don't hold with the old ways, they were still happy to have Lily around.'

'Lily Jenkins Secrets . . .' Crow mused. 'You're suggesting dying people talked to her.'

'Dying people do talk. And what do they talk about? I don't know. Lily Jenkins does. That's how she got her nickname.'

'And you think she might have sat with Sarah Parry?'

'Doesn't live far away. Nothing to lose, sir. Except a bit of breath, walking.'

'It's downhill now,' Crow said, and scrambled to his feet.

CHAPTER 7

Treharne Street boasted a better standard of housing than its neighbouring streets. The houses were still terraced, with no front gardens or walls — those houses were in the Crescent where the bank manager lived — but they had front doors that were recessed so that anyone knocking and waiting for a reply had a small narrow porch in which to wait, free from wind and rain. They were useful for people waiting for buses, though it upset the householders who found their front doorsteps getting muddy before it was time to sand and scrub them again. Sand from Porthcawl, gathered on the day of the usual street outing when everyone crowded onto the bus for the thirty mile journey to the beach, one day each year.

Not that Lily Jenkins had sanded her front step for some time. As Dewi Jones knocked for the third time Crow stood in contemplation of the porch. It was rather shabby, where other porches would be bright and shining, and the decorative wall tiles were yellowing, their *motif* cracked and stained though still discernible as a St George Corpulent engaging in battle with a Dragon distinctly Scrofulent. The brass knocker on the door had not been cleaned in a long while and was badly stained; when Jones knocked yet again the sound echoed as though in an empty house.

'Won't do no good, you know.'

Crow turned around in surprise. The fat little woman standing in the street wore an apron around her ample waist and curlers in her hair, pieces of blue plastic caught up in wisps of greying thinning hair.

'Won't do you no good 'cos she hasn't been out in weeks, hasn't had visitors in months. Still alive, she is, we know that, because we hear her movin' about in the mornin's, getting her cup of tea, and she always takes in the milk. See, gone it is now. I'm Mrs Richards. My husband's foreman in the garage down the road. Live next door, we do.'

Dewi Jones turned to her.

'We'd like to have a word with her.'

'I can see that.' Mrs Richards spoke to Dewi Jones, but her eyes remained fixed on John Crow, openly curious, staring at his bald, domed head and deep-set eyes with utter fascination. 'But she won't answer the door. I tell you, she had a couple of visitors months ago, there was a chap, I remember, didn't know him, think he was from the council or something, but he was the last and no one's been in there since. She comes out late afternoons sometimes, does a bit of shopping up the street, you see, and then it's back in, talk to nobody. Gone funny, you know, that's what everyone's saying. . .She didn't even go around to see Sammy Feeney and that was a surprise.'

'Feeney?' Jones said, puzzled by the reference.

'Well, you know,' Mrs Richards said, giving him a quick flicker of her little blue eyes before staring again at Crow.

'She lays you out, don't she? And when you're on your last legs she's around to keep watch, like. Feeney was an old friend, but she didn't go to him and it's a fact she hasn't been to anyone in months. Funny she's gone. My husband now, he thinks she's on the way out herself and knows it.'

'No one's tried to get in?'

'Few have shouted through the letter box. No good though. She doesn't answer, you know.' She hesitated, glancing again at Dewi Jones. 'Seen you before. You're police aren't you?'

Jones nodded.

'I got a key, see,' the woman said almost reflectively.

Crow spoke for the first time.

'You've got a key and you haven't gone in to see how Mrs Jenkins might be?'

Mrs Richards looked at him as though he were stupid; she bridled a little, folded her arms across her ample bosom.

'Now look here, not my place to go pokin' my nose in there. Neighbours all around here, we visit, just knock and go in you know, but if a door's locked to you, you don't go using keys to get in. Her house, isn't it? Her life. Not our business to go pushing in! Up to her it is. But this key, I've had it for some time, when she got the flu, it was, from the time I used to do some shoppin' for her when she was took to her bed. Tell you the truth, I think she probably forgot I had it, really; I forgot myself, in fact, until recent. But seeing you're police, like, you can have the key, can't you?'

She held it out in her broad hand to Dewi Jones but she directed her statement at John Crow.

'You're that chap from Scotland Yard.'

* * *

Delicacy had to be discarded in discouraging the determined Mrs Richards from entering the house with them. She was remarkably thick-skinned and tenacious, not easily removed from the house once she had set foot in it. Finally, Dewi Jones took her by her red elbow and propelled her out past St George with a firmness bordering on the violent.

She complained bitterly on the pavement about police brutality and she was only wanting to help, then waddled off across the road to tell the other neighbours what she thought of violent police behaviour and it didn't ought to be allowed because she paid her taxes, didn't she? And she remembered Dewi Jones when he didn't have any arse in his trousers.

The house was very quiet when she had gone.

The two policemen walked through the dark passageway with its brown-painted stair banisters and brown-painted wallpaper into the room beyond. It served as a sitting-room, Crow decided; an ancient sagging settee, two easy chairs covered in a brocaded material now considerably faded. Everything was dusty, yet neat, and it was obvious that before Mrs Jenkins had become a complete recluse she had been house-proud. Most Welsh women were, Jones said in an undertone. They walked past the white plastic ducks floating quietly in the glass bowl and entered the kitchen. There was no one there.

No fire burned in the old black-leaded grate and the only food in sight was the loaf of bread on the table and a pot of jam on the Welsh dresser. A bottle of milk stood on the floor by the door leading to the back yard.

'Upstairs?' Jones queried. Crow nodded.

They stood at the foot of the stairs and Dewi Jones called out but there was no reply. Crow sniffed at the air; it had the mustiness of disuse, the smell of decay.

'We'd better go up.'

The stairs proclaimed their presence in loud creaking complaint, and there was a layer of dust on carpet and banisters that marked their progress, hand and foot. On the narrow landing the two men hesitated, Jones called again, there was no reply, but both men heard the creaking of springs, the shifting of a body on a bed. Dewi Jones opened the door to the second room.

For a moment they could see little, for the room was almost in darkness with heavy shades drawn across the window. At last, from the light filtering in from the landing, they were able to make out the woman half-sitting in the bed, propped up against her pillows.

'Mrs Jenkins? Are you all right?' Dewi Jones asked, and stepped forward.

Lily Jenkins made no reply.

She stared straight ahead of her, eyes sunken in wrinkled cheeks, wisps of hair hanging from under a black greasy beret pulled down low over her forehead. She was lying under sheets and blankets, but she was not wearing night clothes; her dress, high-buttoned to the throat, was black and of some age. She had been a big, muscular woman but she had wasted away and the fingers that picked at the coverlet were lean and bony, waiting for death. She seemed unaware of the presence of the two policemen.

'Are you all right, Mrs Jenkins? Do you need a doctor?'

She made no reply, but simply stared vacantly into space, ignoring the two men, even if she were aware of their intrusion into her house. Crow looked around him and shivered. It was strangely cold in this house.

'I think she does need a doctor. She's wasting away.' He hesitated, looking at Jones. 'It's obvious we'll not be able to question her in any way, but I think one of us had better stay with her for the moment. You'd better go and arrange for a doctor to come; I'll wait here till you return.'

Dewi Jones looked doubtfully at Mrs Jenkins, and then again at Crow.

'You be all right?'

It was a strange question to ask and he seemed immediately confused that he should have asked it, for there was no possibility of physical danger in this room. But the atmosphere in the house had affected him in the way it had affected Crow; Mrs Jenkins had laid out many old men and women in her time but now she was waiting for her own layer-out. It was a cold, uncomfortable, eerie house and her presence itself was unnerving. But Crow smiled faintly, nodded his head.

'I'll be all right. Away you go. I'll wait until you get back. But lock the front door behind you — I don't want Mrs Richards and the others crowding in here.'

Dewi Jones hesitated, glanced again at Mrs Jenkins, then turned and left the room. His step was heavy on the stairs, and when he banged the door behind him, leaving the house, the echoes seemed to hang for minutes in the still air of the bedroom.

Crow stood just inside the door, waiting quietly. There was nothing to be done. As far as he could see Mrs Jenkins was undernourished, half starved. Perhaps she had 'gone funny' as Mrs Richards suggested, and was waiting for her time to end. But she needed a doctor and then, probably, hospital. A policeman, asking questions, that was the last thing she needed.

She was still staring in front of her into the darkness.

The air smelled bad, fusty, and thick. Crow left the door open behind him, letting in some light and air, and walked towards the window. He pulled aside the heavy shades, careful not to allow too much light to strike into the room, and tried to open the old-fashioned sash windows. They were firm, could not be moved. He stepped back, let the shades fall back into place, and turned back towards the bed.

The voice startled him, sent a crawling feeling up his spine.

'I know you.'

The voice had a light quality, dry, the sound of leaves whispering along a wind-blown pavement, scurrying into dark corners and whirling about, clicking and scratching and scraping, but her lips hardly seemed to have moved. But her eyes had; where they had been vacant and staring ahead of her now they were alive, glittering in the dimness, watching Crow as he moved towards her. Her body remained still, her fingers no longer picking at the coverlet, but her eyes were bright, almost excited, eager as a lover's.

'Seen you many times, I have. Saw you when it was my brother's turn, that was the first time, 1933, was it?'

Crow stood still, puzzled for a moment, not knowing what to say but guessing the old woman was lapsing into delirium, was seeing visions.

'Many times . . .' Lily Jenkins whispered again. 'All those people, and most of them was afraid, you see. That's why I used to sit with them, hold a hand, give a cup of warm milk, sometimes with a little drop of whisky in it, talk to them in the darkness and listen to what they had to say, all their troubles and their worries. Never told on them of course, no matter anyway, they went. But they needed me, you see. Had to have me there. They was afraid, that was it, they was afraid of *you*. I was, really, first time. But not after. They was afraid of you so I used to sit there between you and them until it was time and they went and you had gone too and then I put them to peace, like, closed their old eyes. But no one sitting with me, now, is there? Don't need anyone, see. 'Cos I seen you, already, often enough. Nothin' to be afraid of in you, is there . . .?'

John Crow was cold. He stood there, incapable of speech as the old woman whispered on, her eyes seeming to burn with a fierce light in the dimness.

'Never seen you so clear, mind, not so clear as now. You used to be shadowy, hanging about just behind my shoulder somehow, not standing there in front of me. But there it is, different you see, when it's my turn. That's what you come to say, isn't it? I don't mind. Been too long it has. These last months . . . And now, no one to talk to, except you. No one to tell all those stories to, about my brother, and my uncle, about Tom Thomas and Edwina, and Sally Rees and all those others, their names I nearly forget now, all of them told me things and I never told anyone, except once and that was bad and wrong and I'd never do it again, I promised anyway, but with you it's different 'cos you don't tell anyone. And they don't even see you till now, do they? But nothing to be frightened of, anyway. Your eyes, like, they're not what they put in paintings . . . You got kind eyes, really, I can see them, all soft and sympathetic, like. I wonder if all those people saw your eyes like that, in the end. Must have helped, if they did. Wouldn't be afraid no more then, would they, wouldn't be afraid of you no more . . .'

She thought he was Death.

There had been many occasions during his adult life when John Crow had been made aware of his appearance and of people's reaction to it. For some, first acquaintance had been a matter of surprise, for others, amusement. His long, bony frame, awkward wrists, skinny body, bald domed head and deep-set eyes beside a prominent nose could hardly be ignored, but this was the first time that anyone had looked at him, seen him, and taken him for the Old Reaper. It was an experience he would rather have missed; it left him cold, shaken, though strangely enough, not annoyed. He had come to terms with his appearance over the years and could accept that people reacted to it; it helped now, but Lily Jenkins still left him disturbed.

She whispered on in her dry-leaves voice and he hardly heard the words; he saw the shining of her eyes, life in the old husk of her body, and he stood stock-still, listening, not understanding, shaking slightly at the thought of all those people, just names now, who had lived and died over the years and whose memories had been stored up in the mind of Lily Jenkins Secrets. She had sat and comforted them and they had talked about the lusty youth they had seen and lost, about the anxieties that middle age had brought to them, about the souring disappointments of a life slipping by with little or nothing to show, children gone, reason gone, life going. She knew it all, Mrs Jenkins, knew it but had never spoken it.

'. . . I used to think one time it was like bein' a Catholic priest and listening to all those confessions just like Father Power in Treorchy Catholic Church and not telling a word about what was said. Proud I was, proud about it, because a lot of people used to ask me, greedy people who wanted something and lonely people who wished they'd heard such words or people who were just curious, but I never said a word to any one of them. Not about Joan Edwards and her goings on, John Willie Monkey taking those bets in the street, or Sergeant Carter's Christmas chickens from the bookmaker down in Gelli, no, I never said none of it to anyone, not even about Sarah Parry . . .'

She stopped suddenly, for Crow had moved in an involuntary gesture of surprise. Sarah Parry, Gran Parry, Ceinwen Williams's grandmother. She had been the reason for Crow's visit and he had almost forgotten it, yet Lily Jenkins had mentioned her name now. The eyes glistened at him in the darkened bedroom and Lily Jenkins seemed to tense under the bedclothes as though she had become aware of his sudden surge of excitement and surprise.

But there was more than a sudden tension on her part: there was a shrinking too, a cowering into the protection of the covering blankets.

'It was only the once,' she whispered anxiously, 'only the once . . . about Sarah Parry, what she told me . . .'

John Crow loomed over her, his face grey and bony, threatening and deathly in the dimness. She felt the threat even though in reality it was not there; she felt Death's disapproval of her conduct, of the looseness of her tongue and she began to speak quickly but coherently, explaining, arguing . . .

'Sarah Parry was old and she was dying and she began to ramble like old people do, like I'm doing now when we face you like this. She told me about being a girl in Treherbert when there was hardly any houses and the trees were all on the hillsides like they are coming back now but different trees, pine trees now. And she told me about her husband Tom, good man he was . . . But she was awful worried, she was, those last days about her Ceinwen, wondering what would become of her, especially workin' for that man Martin Evans down in Pentre. And she told me all about it, all about it . . .'

In a voice matching her own for dryness Crow asked huskily 'What did Sarah Parry tell you? About Ceinwen and Martin Evans?'

Lily Jenkins whimpered like a dog about to be beaten by a threatening master.

'I didn't want to talk about it,' she cried, 'and now, you want me to. She didn't tell me much, just hints first, but the whole story later. She talked for a long time, weak she was, lying in bed holding my hand so I could give her strength, she talked about her daughter Annie and what a wayward one *she* was, married a good man but always gave him trouble, ended up going off with a Yank to America. There's scandal it was at the time, but it was over and done and Ceinwen was soon with her, lovely child she was, so quiet and good, not like her mother, brazen she was. And then she told me about the way Ceinwen went to London to work and she was sad until Ceinwen wrote to say she had met a lovely man and she was getting married and was bringing her husband home to meet Sarah. She was a bit sad, you know, that Ceinwen should have married without coming for a big splash of a marriage in the chapel back in Treherbert, but the young ones felt they couldn't wait, see, in love they were, and so they were married in London, in a registry, and they came down a week later to meet Gran Parry. And she recognized him. . .'

'*Recognized* him?'

Lily Jenkins quivered. Her hand moved away from the coverlet, brushed a lock of hair, tucked it back into her black beret and nodded. She peered up at Crow, a real terror seizing her now.

'Aye, well, she recognized him because he was so like his father, you see, and she knew his father, he was a friend of her daughter's husband, friend of Annie's husband he was, and a friend of Annie too come to that, and she recognized him and she was upset, she cried for days, and Martin went away and Ceinwen went away too, and then she carne back later when Sarah Parry was poorly and then she stayed with her. But she was so worried when she died, with that Martin Evans back in Pentre and Ceinwen working for him, though Ceinwen was a good girl, never did anything wrong, you know, never since!'

Crow hesitated. The old woman was shivering in real terror and he felt that to question her further would distress her, but the picture still confused him, even though the suspicion grew with every word he heard, the suspicion that he was now close to the real motives for Martin Evan's confession.

'Mrs Jenkins,' he said, 'you're telling me this—'

'I told you, I didn't want to talk about it and I promised not to but with you it's different, because you know it all, don't you?'

'Promised? Promised Mrs Parry, you mean?'

The brass knocker on the door downstairs was hammered loudly and Lily Jenkins started up in the bed, lean hands clutching the covers. Her blue eyes were wide now, the terror plain to see.

'Promised her, and promised him after I told him!' She glared wildly around her. 'I didn't want to tell him, but I did, because I had to, didn't I!'

The knocker sounded again and Mrs Jenkins leapt up in bed, drawing her knees up under her, cowering against the bed head.

'That's not the man, is it? He said he wouldn't come again, not after I told him and promised to stay quiet after. He said he'd leave me alone then. But if that's him downstairs you got to take me before he comes up because I'm afraid of him. I know you, seen you lots of times, and your eyes are kind but I'm afraid of him. Don't let him come, not before you—'

'Mrs Jenkins!' Crow leaned forward, put his hand on the old woman's shoulder, and shook her gently. 'It's all right. No one will come unless I allow them to come. Be quiet, be peaceful. Everything will be all right.'

'I told him,' she mumbled, calming somewhat under Crow's touch. 'He made me tell him, first time I ever told secrets. Told him about Sarah Parry's secrets.'

'Tell me, Mrs Jenkins,' Crow said quietly, but urgently. 'Tell me about her secrets, and tell me about this man.'

The hammering below started again, insistently.

* * *

The queue for seats at the hearing before the Crown Court had begun to form in the early hours of the morning and when Crow arrived it already extended far down the street. He made himself known to the policeman at the doors and he was allowed in immediately.

He found Warlock and the prosecuting counsel, Weir in the chamber beyond the robing-room. As Crow came in Warlock looked up doubtfully, but Weir rose with an impatient grimace.

'Have you got the papers?'

Crow nodded and handed the file he carried to Weir.

'I'm sorry I was held up. But I've carried out all the necessary checks. I think we could prove all we now suspect.'

Jason Warlock tapped his fingers on the table in front of him, and squinted down his long nose.

'Detective Chief Inspector Crow. We've met before, I believe. Across a courtroom once or twice. But never in such. . .ah. . .intriguing circumstances. All most mysterious. My friend Weir asks to see me here before the jury is empanelled, but declines to say why.'

Weir waved the file after his brief inspection of it.

'Fact is, we want a postponement. Want you to agree to our request to adjourn for further investigation.'

Warlock's eyebrows rose. Icily, he said, 'You must be mad. To start with, Mr Justice Carroll is unlikely to agree to it, but I certainly could not. Damn it, Weir, you've had long enough to prepare your case against Martin Evans. You came into the magistrates court ill-prepared for the preliminary enquiry, but I'm damned if I'll now give you assistance in making a better case than the one you've got, by agreeing to adjournment. I presume that is why you're asking for more time — to plug yet more gaps in your case?'

'Not quite that simple,' Weir said grumpily. 'More facts have now come into our possession, and they place a slightly different complexion on the case. They don't detract from Evans's guilt, as I see it, but they do bring in a complication we need to sort out. About motive.'

'If you have any information,' Warlock said coolly, eyeing the file, 'you are duty bound to make it available to the defence.'

Weir handed him the file without speaking. Warlock smiled, read it through quickly, then went back and read it again with more care.

'All verified?' he said sharply when he had finished his perusal.

'All verified,' Crow said in a firm tone. 'The source of much of the information will be in a position to testify, having made a remarkable recovery now she knows she is not in fact going to die and I am just a policeman, not the Old Reaper himself.'

A glimmer of amusement appeared in Warlock's eyes but he did not smile. He handed the file back to Weir, thinking hard.

'I think we should go see my client,' he suggested at last.

* * *

Martin Evans looked pale. There were dark patches under his eyes that suggested he had not been sleeping well and he seemed thinner. He was still polite and reserved in his greeting, however. Crow noted the anxiety that lurked at the back of his eyes nevertheless.

'Martin, we've had some rather . . . ah . . . interesting information which puts rather a different complexion on things. What I want you to do. . .' Warlock paused, looked at Crow, then leaned back in his chair. 'Perhaps it would be more fitting if it came from you,' he suggested.

Crow inclined his head and looked carefully at Martin Evans. The anxiety was there, so he decided to come straight to the point.

'We know the truth, Martin.'

Martin Evans stiffened, but said nothing.

'We know the truth about your motives, and it could be it will change the situation considerably. On the other hand, it may not.'

Martin Evans coughed, cleared his throat. Coldly, he said, 'I don't know what you're talking about.'

Crow sighed.

'We've got the facts, Martin, but to persuade you this is no trick I'll go over them. The thing started, as you well know, just after you were born. Your father, Alan Stark, and your mother Jean were friendly with Fred and Annie Williams, who had a daughter, Ceinwen, a few years younger than you. After the Starks took you to Canada they continued to write for a couple of years and then it died away. Fred and Annie got divorced, Fred died, Ceinwen was brought up by her grandmother Sarah Parry, you grew up in Canada. When your father died you came looking for Ceinwen to give her the legacy your father had left her in his will. You found Ceinwen in London, fell in love with her, married her.'

Martin Evans leaned forward, his eyes hard. 'I don't know why you're going over all this again. What's the point?'

'The point is, when you came to the Rhondda to meet Gran Parry she saw your father in you. And she broke up your marriage.'

'I don't see—'

'You and Ceinwen didn't break it up by quarrelling or discovering you were incompatible. It broke up the day you met Sarah Parry. She told you the truth, told you what Annie Williams had told her before she went to America. She told you that you and Ceinwen should not have married. . .ever.'

'Damn you, I—'

'She told you that Ceinwen was your half-sister.'

* * *

It was all there in the papers on his knee, the statements, the affidavits, the reasons. Annie Williams had always been a girl of an accommodating disposition; she had been pregnant when Fred Williams married her but the baby had been stillborn. She and Fred had been friendly with Alan and Jean Stark. Alan was a handsome man, and when Jean Stark had been at home with the baby Martin there had been occasions when Alan had been able to slip away to meet Annie. When Ceinwen was born, Fred thought he was the father. Annie knew otherwise.

She had told her mother, Sarah Parry, before she went triumphantly to the States. Ceinwen was Alan Stark's child.

Martin and Ceinwen had the same father.

It was not until 1942 that Fred had learned the truth: he had divorced Annie but he had not turned away from Ceinwen. He had loved the child too much to discard her at that point, and he had looked after her as his own until he died. But he was never in contact with the Starks after he learned the truth.

Alan Stark had certainly been aware that Ceinwen was his daughter. He and Jean had had only the one son, and perhaps he had always longed secretly for a daughter; it would have accounted for the fact that his will named her as a beneficiary. But it also promoted the fateful meeting between two young people who were closely related but did not know it — until they married, came back to the Rhondda for a grandmother's blessing and then discovered the shattering truth.

'We were stunned,' Martin Evans said woodenly. 'Gran Parry sat there with a face like iron, as though she blamed us for doing something evil, but how could we have regarded it as evil? We were married, we wanted to spend the rest of our lives together. We were so happy — and now we were crushed by the realisation that we could never marry legally, never be . . . lovers. *But we were in love!*'

He sat in front of Crow and the two silent lawyers. His face was marked with suffering and frustration, past and present, and his eyes were clouded.

'I wanted to blame someone, you know what I mean? I wanted to blame Gran Parry for telling us, for if she had remained silent who was to know about it? I wanted to blame my father, for being Ceinwen's father in the first instance, for never telling me later. But again, where was the need for him to tell me? She was to all intents and purposes merely the daughter of a friend. I looked at Ceinwen and saw the agony in her face, the fearfulness because we had done wrong — unwittingly perhaps, but we had done wrong — and Gran Parry herself, she emphasised it with all her strict, strait-laced views, she drove it home. . .I almost went out of my mind.'

He shook his head. 'But then, when I calmed down I knew there was only one thing to do. I had to leave, I had to get away from there. So I went back to London, Ceinwen came up a few days later, we talked it all over calmly and rationally and we agreed what had to be done. That was it, then. I went up to Newcastle, took a post with a firm of solicitors, and after a while Ceinwen went back to the Rhondda.'

'And then you met Donna?' Crow asked.

Martin Evans nodded. His craggy features were ashen.

'When I look back it's as though I was dogged with evil luck. Of all the women to pick — Donna! But I was lonely, she was a good-looking woman and she could charm the birds off the trees. She was working there in the office, I took her out and . . . well, she wanted marriage and so we got married.'

'But you never got an annulment of the first marriage to Ceinwen Williams.'

'God, man, can't you see what it would have meant?'

Anger flushed Evans's cheeks as he glared at Crow and the two barristers.

'I couldn't go to court and ask for an annulment on the basis of my blood relationship to Ceinwen! They would have crucified her, in the Press, in the valley, it could never have been kept quiet! I didn't even dare ask for a divorce, or ask her to petition for one, because again there was always the chance that the real reason for the divorce would emerge. It was an impossible situation, so I took the easy way out . . . I lied to the Registrar, I went through a ceremony of marriage . . .'

'But you were still in love with Ceinwen,' Crow suggested.

The anger that had flared in Evans's face died again. He looked down miserably at his hands.

'That was the problem, right from the beginning. It's easy to blame Donna for what happened, but I can't do that, not entirely. It may be that if I'd been able to give her the love she wanted, maybe things would have turned out differently. Maybe she wouldn't have gone off the rails again, wouldn't have started affairs, and wouldn't have got involved with that man Klein. But I wasn't able to give her love, not even affection. I could give her little, for as soon as I married her I felt resentful. It should have been Ceinwen who was with me, not Donna. I felt guilty about being with her because I loved Ceinwen, I felt guilty in loving Ceinwen, my whole life was a mess and I drifted, until suddenly Donna was leaving me, the Klein papers were missing . . . Again, I could have blamed Donna, pointed out she'd probably taken them, but I was too low, too dispirited, too unhappy. And I wanted to be near Ceinwen. I couldn't bear to be parted from her any more. So I accepted my partners' arguments about negligence, left the firm, used what money I had left to buy Morgan and Enoch and I started in business as an estate agent, under the name Martin Evans. Then I asked Ceinwen to come work for me.'

'That must have been playing with fire,' Crow said quietly.

Martin Evans shook his head.

'Not really. Gran Parry certainly saw it that way but Ceinwen understood. She knew I loved her as she did me: she knew I'd do nothing to hurt her, and she knew that at least this way we'd be together much of the time. It would hurt, of course, but it was more bearable than the hurt we felt being apart. And that's the way it's been these years. Together, and yet not together . . . but it was the best we could make of our condition.'

'Until Donna appeared. And she spoiled it all?'

'I'd never told Ceinwen about Donna,' Evans said fiercely. 'You've got to remember that. I never told her because she would have been unhappy at the thought of me having lived with someone else, having gone through a ceremony of marriage, and that's all I've wanted to do — protect her. She could never have taken the gossip if the truth had come out.'

Crow understood. He thought of Ceinwen Williams, small, shy, nervous, diffident, the kind of woman scandal would sear. He understood Martin Evans's motives.

'So when Donna wrote to me—'

'She wrote to you?'

'The envelope you found in my desk — it contained a blackmail demand. Pay two thousand pounds or the story of my bigamous marriage and incestuous relationship with

Ceinwen would come out. And then she phoned me. She said she was coming to the valley, wanted to speak to me.'

Warlock stirred uneasily. He moved forward as though to position himself nearer Martin Evans. Crow ignored him.

'The envelope you received-when did it arrive?'

'End of May, I think. I'm not exactly sure"

'And Donna sent it?'

Evans frowned.

'I suppose so. I mean, there was nothing to suggest it was her; I mean, it was made up with pieces of words cut out of newspapers, even the address on the envelope itself. But when she came along later and made her demands I assumed it was her letter. Anyway, she arrived that night—
'

'When?'

'June the 6th. She didn't come to the office, I didn't want her to be seen, so I arranged to meet her on the track, at the back of the office, leading up to the Bwylffa Pit. She was waiting there, we began to walk up the track—'

'I think that will do, Martin.' Warlock smiled coldly towards Crow and Weir. 'I think that's as far as we need go now. I assume you have what you wanted?'

Martin Evans seemed suddenly startled, as he was made aware he had been talking too much. Crow saw the lawyer in him take over from the lover and he cursed under his breath.

'There are a few more questions I'd like to ask,' Crow said stiffly.

'But not now, not of my client,' Warlock replied. 'I do not consider it in his best interests to answer such further questions as you may have until I have first consulted with him. We do not want a repetition of the first occasion, when a confession was obtained by doubtful means.'

"The means were in no way doubtful,' Crow said, 'and I assure you, if I can ask just a few more questions which are in no sense incriminating of your client I should be able to—'

'To clearly tie up loose ends for the prosecution,' Warlock interrupted. 'I can't allow that, Inspector.'

'What about the adjournment?' Weir asked fiercely.

Warlock smiled; it was a wolfish smile, mocking in its air.

'Well, now, it's as I said before. The question is hardly one I can answer. It's up to the judge. But it does seem to me that the problems are all yours. Now we know more clearly the motives of my client—'

'Now we know his motives,' Weir interrupted, 'it makes much stronger the case for murder!'

'I disagree,' Warlock said, exchanging a quick glance with Martin Evans. 'His motivations were of the highest. He wanted to protect Ceinwen Williams from scandal; he would have done anything to save her from valley gossip. Even face a charge of murder. All right, if you now want to remove the reason for his protection of her, by exposing the incestuous union, or the bigamous marriage, in open court, you also remove his necessity to face that confession. For the defence can show — and I'll plead it hard, believe me — that the confession was worthless, motivated as it was by his situation. I don't know a jury that wouldn't be moved by the plea, do you?'

'Warlock—' Weir began warningly, but Crow interrupted him.

'I think the matter may be capable of solution in another way,' he said. 'I can ask someone else the questions I have in mind.'

'Be my guest,' Warlock said, still smiling. 'Ask your questions of anyone, except my client Martin Evans. I'm not yet quite ready to throw him to the lions!'

* * *

The witness-room was sparsely furnished and guarded by a uniformed constable who stepped aside smartly to admit John Crow. The witnesses for the prosecution, in spite of the fact they had all appeared at the preliminary hearing and were now known to each other, retained a separateness that emphasised they were thrown here together by chance, rather than by inclination. James Klein stood completely aloof, staring out of the window towards the civic buildings. Jack Scales stood near the far window, smoking nervously. Of the others, only the enquiry agent Edward Skene and the fish-fryer Dai Davies seemed to have found something in common, something to talk about. They sat side by side at the table, talking in a desultory fashion. John Crow walked across to them, drew a chair up, sat down beside them.

Dai Davies looked at him rather doubtfully, offered him a cigarette and then, when Crow declined, lit one for himself and for Skene.

'They'll be getting the jury sworn in soon,' Crow said.

'Aye. The sooner the bloody better,' Teddy Skene said angrily. 'I got a living to earn.'

'Me too,' Davies agreed.

'You two know each other — apart from this case, I mean?'

Dai Davies looked quickly at Skene, half grinned, and shrugged his shoulders.

'Well, yes and no, like. I mean, I didn't know Teddy first time we crossed paths in the magistrates' hearing, but later I got to thinking and sure enough, when he got time to have a chat later we discovered that we did know each other from way back. Teddy here, he went to school in the Rhondda; like I did. Didn't you, boy?'

Skene nodded, scratched his thinning hair and grinned.

'That's right. Me and Dai here we used to mitch from the junior school in the afternoon, looking for fag ends in the gutter. Stuck a matchstick in them, tried to smoke them. Not very successfully. Hey, long time ago now, Dai.'

'Aye, it is that.'

'You lived in Treorchy, Mr Skene?' Crow asked.

'Treherbert. Only as a kid, though. Never came back to the valley after I spent my time, National Service, in the Army. Settled down in Cardiff I did, but you heard about my—'

'Antecedents, yes, at the preliminary hearing. I heard the evidence you gave.' Crow turned almost casually to Dai Davies. 'I wasn't there to hear your evidence, though.'

Dai Davies opened his eyes wider in affected surprise.

'Don't suppose you needed to, did you? After all, there was my statement to go on, the one I made to the police. And you interviewed me personal, anyway.'

'Ah, yes, that's so. But the trouble is, I understand you changed your story somewhat under cross-examination by counsel for the defence.'

'That twisty bastard!' Davies looked suddenly glum. 'He was a right one, that man wasn't he? And I suppose he's on again for this hearing as well. Don't like him, don't mind telling you that. He was rough with me. Same with you as well, wasn't he Teddy?'

'You can say that again,' Skene replied and glanced at Crow. 'But what's the problem, Inspector? You want us both to go over our statements again with you?'

Crow smiled and shook his head.

'It's not that. I'm just interested in the fact that Mr Warlock seemed to shake Mr Davies here, more than a little, over the question of dates. Perhaps you can explain that to me, Mr Davies?'

Dai Davies could, but he didn't want to. He lowered his eyes, considered the matter silently for a few seconds. He began to chew nervously at his lip. Regret rustled in his voice as he said, 'He got me to say . . . well, he just caught me on the hop, that's all. Won't catch me the second time, I tell you that.'

'Catch you? How did he catch you, Mr Davies?' Crow asked, with concern in his voice.

Doubtfully, Davies looked at him to discover whether the concern was genuine. He glanced at Skene for assistance, but none was forthcoming; Skene merely seemed puzzled, and somewhat indifferent. Davies sighed.

'Well, he just got me confused, that's all.'

'Over the dates?'

'That's right. Over the dates. In my statement I said I saw that woman on the hill, about ten in the evening of June 6th. That barrister, he chased me up on that one. Got me confused.'

'But you were clear enough in your statement,' Crow said wonderingly. 'You stated you could easily verify the date, because it was a Tuesday and that accounted for your not being in the shop, but out on the hill, on the way back from the Club or wherever.'

'That's so. That's the way it was,' Davies said with a hint of aggression in his tones.

'So how did Mr Warlock disturb you, confuse you?'

When Davies shrugged, looked uncomfortable, Crow went on, 'He suggested that you might be wrong about the dates, didn't he? He pointed out that according to information he had received your shop was *open* only on the Monday of the week in question, that it was closed for the rest of the time that week and so it was *possible* that it was not the 6th of June on which you saw Donna Stark, but the 7th, or the 8th or—'

'If you know what he suggested, why do you ask me now?' Davies demanded belligerently.

'Because I know you've been lying right from the beginning about Donna Stark,' Crow said.

Skene swivelled his head in surprise to stare at Crow and the movement caught the attention of Jack Scales near the far window. He looked towards the small group at the table and he frowned. But Dai Davies sat rigid, his eyes glaring, his mouth open but seemingly petrified. The colour had faded from his face, leaving his skin grey, dead-looking.

'Wha . . . what the hell do you mean by that?'

Crow smiled, and shook his head.

'Come on, Mr Davies, it's a bit late to put on that sort of act. You know and I know that your story about Donna Stark has never rung true. We never followed it up because it fitted well enough with the facts we knew then, but since more information has come to light—'

'What information?' Skene asked wonderingly.

'I'll come to that in a moment,' Crow said. 'But first of all, you *did* lie didn't you, Mr Davies?'

'I don't know what you're talking about,' Dai Chippo said sullenly.

'You know exactly what I'm talking about. You've testified you saw Mrs Stark on the sixth, and support it by reference to the Tuesday closing. But Warlock showed you could be mistaken . . . I suspect you *were* . . . or otherwise you were deliberately *misstating* the situation.'

'The ticket in her pocket—'

'Forget the ticket in her pocket. What about the brooch she wore? You said you recognized it down in the shaft—if so, you must have seen it at close quarters! And why did it make such an impression on you for you to remember it, months later? Before you say anything more, let me warn you, if we press matters, I'm pretty sure we'll be able to find out what you were doing on the *Tuesday* night. What I want to know is, when *did* you see Donna Stark and in what circumstances?'

Dai Chippo was silent for a while. He stared vacantly at Teddy Skene but he did not see him; his eyes were glazed as though he were looking inward at himself, and not liking very much what he saw.

'I suppose that chap Warlock will be questioning me on this anyway,' he said reluctantly. 'So I might as well get it over with, now, with you. But you got to understand my . . . my motives.'

'I'm listening,' Crow said calmly.

'It's Margaret, really, my wife you know. Ask anyone, she makes my life hell. Or would, if she could entirely, but she's got to have her off times too, so she goes to Ponty market and so on, Tuesdays. That's when I'm able to get some free time . . .' He hesitated, considering whether to continue, but decided to put a brave face on it. 'If you was to ask around I suppose there'd be some snoopy devils who'd tell you about a couple of women in Ton . . . but the thing is, I had to break out once in a while, you know? And they was always willin' we used to fix it up when they came into the shop. Funny that, women customers is pushovers to a chap in a shop . . . Anyway, that particular week I wasn't able to go to this woman on Tuesday—'

'Her name?'

'Aw, come on . . .' Dar Chippo hesitated, then shrugged his shoulders, grinned at Skene in a half-hearted fashion, pulled a diary out of his pocket and scribbled a name on a sheet, tore it out and passed it to Crow.

'You understand, Teddy.'

Skene grinned slyly, in a conspiratorial fashion.

'Only making sure you can go back there and don't warm her sheets before I find time to get back to her.'

'Go on,' said Crow, reading the name.

'Thing was, on the Tuesday I had to visit Margaret at Church Village Hospital: she was in having her foot done—bloody tight shoes, you know what women are like—and then I went to the Club but come Thursday I'd fixed up to go around to this bird whose name you got there. I went down about seven and, damn me, her husband wasn't off on the night shift after all but was home with his feet up. I tell you, I was annoyed, damn frustrated, I'd been looking forward to it all week, so I . . . well, I went and got canned.'

He frowned, bit at the skin of his right thumb, spat out a small piece of grey skin.

'You got to remember, it's what accounts for it, I never done nothing like this before.'

'Like what?'

'Well . . . I came out of the Red Lion about ten, pretty well under. I was still boiling for Sal — that woman, and I was randy as hell. The shop was closed, no one home, a cold bed waiting and I was like an old ram. Then I saw this woman walking down the hill.'

He looked up, protestingly, to Crow. 'Now believe me, I never done anything like it before. I told you, customers come into the shop, you chat them up, bit of sly dirty talk and you're away, I tell you. So I never had the need before. But there I was, randy as hell, there she was, a stranger, walking alone down the hill—'

'You accosted her?' Crow asked coldly.

Dai Chippo nodded miserably.

'That's it. Walked up, put my arm around her – you could see how drunk I was — asked her straight out. Stupid, I was. Finesse, hell! But she swore at me, you know, gave me a right mouthful. I was surprised. She seemed smart, a nice piece, but the language she used I only heard before among the pit lads—and not even much of that. Made me angry in a way, so I jeered at her, stayed with her as she walked down the hill, and then when we came near the lamps at the bottom there, up above the Square, I saw her face. She had a swelling under her left eye. Somebody'd given her a real thump.'

He glanced at Skene and then back to Crow.

'Not me, I swear. But someone had thumped her, and she was shaking, either because I was trying to chat her up or because the thump had shaken her up, I don't know. But I saw that, and I saw the brooch; I sort of stared at the brooch to avoid seeing that swelling, you know, after the first moment? I said she seemed to need a feller to look after her, but she wasn't taking that line, and I got mad, grabbed at her and shook her — I know, it was a rotten thing to do — and she started to cry. I left her alone then, swearing at me. I went back up the hill, she went to the Square. That was it.'

'You didn't see her again?'

'Not till I saw her in the shaft.' Dai Chippo rubbed a nervous hand across his mouth. 'But that brooch . The thing was, you remember what it was like? Oval, lightning bolt through it. I tell you, I was pretty tight that night and next day I didn't remember much but that bloody brooch kept coming back to me at night when I was dreaming, you know? I knew I'd done something wrong, uncharacteristic like, but it took me a long time to get the pieces in place, but that's the whole story. But that brooch, bloody phallic symbol like, it was like it kept coming back into my mind to reproach me. . .and then, damn me, there it was glittering at me in the shaft! I could have been sick right there, because it brought it back, and I never approached a woman like that before, tried to force myself on her, but I was drunk . . .'

'Why did you still stick to the story about seeing her on the sixth?'

'Easiest thing to do,' Dai Davies replied, 'I mean, at first I wasn't sure anyway, and then there was the ticket in her pocket, and later Evans said he done her in on the sixth, so what was the odds? Should I rock the boat, say I saw her alive on the eighth and then have Margaret asking what the hell I was doing accosting women while she was in hospital for a minor op on her bloody big toe? Not likely! So I went along with things. But I don't see it's important anyway.'

'I do,' Crow said.

Skene hitched forward in his chair. 'How so? If Evans says he killed her and is wrong about the date, so what? Unless . . . unless he's withdrawn his confession?'

Crow shook his head.

'He's not done that, not yet anyway, and his counsel wouldn't let me question him further on the matter of dates, in case more damaging information would come out.'

'So what's the problem?' Skene said, leaning back and smiling expansively. He looked up, grinned at Jack Scales as the man approached slowly. 'Nothing's changed, really.'

'But it has,' Crow said. He looked at Skene, Scales and Dai Chippo. 'The problem all along has been to get valley people to talk freely, but the most tight-lipped of all has talked at last. Mrs Lily Jenkins.'

Dai Chippo grinned.

'Lily Jenkins Secrets? What the hell has she got to do with this?'

'A great deal,' Crow said calmly. 'After all, she as good as told me who killed Donna Stark.'

* * *

The three men stared at him in shock. It was Jack Scales who spoke first. He stepped forward, glared at Crow, his handsome face marked with anger.

'It's Martin Evans who killed her. He's bloody well confessed to it!'

'Ah, yes, but why did he confess? Get the answer to that and immediately the validity of that confession becomes suspect. You see, Martin Evans is a bigamist and also contracted an incestuous marriage—'

'He *what*?' Dai Chippo gasped.

Crow stared at him with massive calm. Slowly and coldly he said, 'I would not discuss the matter with you but for the fact that it's bound to come out now, it'll have to be made public in the circumstances. But the facts, briefly, are these. Martin Evans, or Stark as he was then known, married Ceinwen Williams, his half-sister. Her grandmother told them the truth; they parted, Evans later married Donna, and then they also broke up.'

'*Ceinwen Williams*?' Dai Chippo shook his head. 'That little mouse? I don't believe it.'

Crow grimaced.

'Didn't the gossips in your shop ever wonder about their relationship, working together, never seeing each other at other times, a bachelor in Ton, a spinster in—'

'I just thought he was queer,' Dai Chippo protested.

Teddy Skene laughed.

'Twisted mind, you got,' he said. 'But this Lily Jenkins nonsense—'

'No nonsense,' Crow said. 'Serious, and important. Martin Evans received a blackmail letter which asked for money, or threatened to expose his relationship with Ceinwen. That was at the end of May. On the 6th of June Donna went to the valley. Martin Evans says he killed her then. I don't believe he did. He said that just to protect Ceinwen. Now, I think he'll say she came asking him for money, that he mentioned the letter, that she went away in a hurry, and returned two days later, this time making the same demands the letter made. Because in the meanwhile she had learned about Ceinwen, too. Her first visit had been one to threaten him with gossip about the fraud in Newcastle or to persuade him to take her back, but her second visit was made after she had spoken to the other person who knew about Ceinwen, the one who had originally sent the blackmail letter.'

'Another person?' Teddy Skene looked puzzled, glanced around the room at Dai Chippo, Jack Scales and James Klein, still standing near the window, trying to listen to the discussion but attempting to appear otherwise.

'I don't get it. All this about Evans and this first marriage . . . two people knew about it?'

'Donna,' Crow said, 'and the man who killed her. The same man who put the fear of death into Lily Jenkins.'

'Lily Jenkins again,' Scales exclaimed in exasperation. 'Where the hell does she fit in? You keep talking of her and yet—'

'Lily Jenkins is an old woman who lays out, and watches over the dying. She was with Sarah Parry—Ceinwen's grandmother, when she was dying. And she heard about the old lady's anxieties, about Ceinwen's marriage, about her now working for Martin Evans, and the relationship between Ceinwen and Martin was made clear to Lily Jenkins. Mrs Parry knew the secret was safe; Lily Jenkins was not named Secrets for nothing. She had always kept quiet.'

'But she talked to *you*, I suppose,' Skene said sarcastically.

'She talked to me, and to a man from the Council.'

'The what?' Dai Chippo said, grinning.

'Everyone has an Achilles' heel,' Crow said grimly. 'And it's never funny when someone finds out where you are vulnerable. You see, Lily Jenkins had lived in that house ever since she was a young woman—'

'If that was ever!' Dai Chippo said.

Crow ignored the interruption.

'She is getting old, she has spent her life there, she loves that house, it is her security and her haven, her pride, for she used to keep it spick and span. And she had her job — laying-out. Until one day the man who said he was from the Council came to see her. He told her that the lease of that house had never been formally made over to her and the freehold was vested in the Crawshaw estate which had been taken over by the Council. He told her that he was empowered to recommend to the Council that old ladies like herself should be taken to the Old People's Hospital at Llwynypia, to make the house available for letting to young families. He said he would have to make the recommendation, and would do so . . . unless he was able to obtain some information from her.'

Crow paused, looked around at the three men listening to him.

'You three will appreciate what this would mean to an old lady like Mrs Jenkins — accustomed to living in the closed Treherbert community, same faces, same friends, same enemies, and now to be forced down the valley to live out her days in strange surroundings, among strange people. She could not bear it. So she told the man from the Council what he wanted to know and he went away and she has heard nothing since. But she has declined: she no longer goes out to sit with the dying, she no longer cleans her house with pride, she no longer sees her neighbours. Instead, she cowers, half starved, in her bedroom, waiting for the knock on the door that will herald her worst fears becoming realised . . . removal from her house, imprisonment in an old people's home.'

'But this is nonsense,' Skene said hotly. He rubbed his sleeve across his brow and his thinning hair fell forward untidily. 'She could have gone to any lawyer and he'd have told her—'

'She's an old woman,' Crow argued. 'Old, gullible, simple, and a valley woman — people in the valley don't go to solicitors except . . . well, when do they?'

'Bloody never,' Dai Chippo grunted, 'all sharks they are.' He eyed Crow speculatively. 'And I can see how she'd be scared. And scared afterwards too, because she'd told this chap from the Council—'

'She was waiting for Death,' Crow said simply.

Skene stood up abruptly, jammed his hands in his pockets.

'The story sounds stupid to me,' he said harshly. 'An old woman's story? An old layer-out who's always been half-way around the bend? Why, I remember as a kid we used to knock at her door and run away, and sing obscene songs through her letter-box because we knew she was crazy as a coot! I mean, have you checked with the Council, to start with? They'd never send anyone around like that.'

'They didn't.' Crow smiled unpleasantly. 'We checked of course. But we already knew the answer before we asked. No, to say he was from the Council gave the man in question entry, and it gave him power, power to frighten Lily Jenkins. And she got frightened, all right. And he got the information he wanted.'

'And I suppose she gave you his name too,' Skene scoffed. 'What was it? John Jones Devil or something?'

'She didn't have to; she didn't have it of course and she thought she might not recognize him again though I suspect she certainly would, if he faced her again. But let me ask you these questions, Mr Skene. Let us assume Martin Evans received a blackmail letter concerning Ceinwen; that he upbraided Donna with it; that she went back to discover from some source what it was all about; that she and this other man then agreed to work together. He then *drove* her to the Rhondda. That would be on the eighth. It was to be for a second meeting with Evans; she met Evans at the Bwylffa pit head but was terrified when he became enraged, hit her, so that she fell against the wheelhouse. He left her, terrified by the anger and passion she had aroused in him, and as for her, she went down to Pentre where Dai Davies accosted her. When she broke away from Davies, she met her accomplice. Which was when she made her fatal mistake.'

Crow looked around at the silent listening group.

'A poor judge of character, Donna. She had blackmailed James Klein successfully, she tried to blackmail Evans and was surprised and frightened by the violence of his reaction. . .she simply had not read his character aright. And she certainly had misread the character of her accomplice. I imagine she had probably recovered some of her poise, after Davies was got rid of. She told her accomplice that she wasn't prepared to keep after Evans—the man was dangerously violent, almost crazed in his fury. But her accomplice was also angered. He felt he could go on without her, target Evans alone. But Donna, she said she'd still need money, to go away and let him do what he wanted with Evans and his secret.'

Crow shook his head sadly.

'It was a stupid thing to do, and yet in character for Donna. She had come so far, blackmail was the ladder she'd used in the past, now she was telling this man she'd go away, let him press Evans for money, as long as he first paid *her* to go away. . .and keep quiet. It may have seemed reasonable enough to her, but it was not reasonable to him. He calculated that if he paid her once, she would be a never-ending drain upon him. Evans had scared her, but how long would that fear last? If *he* scared her, how long would *that* last, in turn? Donna was unreliable, he was on to a good thing with Evans, it could go on for years, a regular source of income, and now Donna was spoiling everything. As he milked Evans, so Donna would milk him. It was something he couldn't stand for. . .and even if he didn't press Evans for money Donna still held out a threat to him. So he killed her.'

There was a short, tense silence. The door at the far end of the room opened and Detective-Inspector Dewi Jones came in. As he walked forward towards them Crow nodded, and smiled.

'I'm just putting them in the picture, Inspector. I'm explaining that the killer maybe tried to frighten Donna in the first instance, as Evans had frightened her, but either way, whether accidentally or deliberately, he succeeded in killing her. Disposal was then the problem . . .'

'So he thought, why not the shaft?' Jones added. 'Dump her there, have her disappear completely.'

'Forget her, the whole unhappy episode, write it off to experience,' Crow continued. 'That's how it was, we believe. A lot of assumptions, I admit, but they're what we're working on, because we're convinced Evans did not murder his wife and I think he'll tell us she walked down that hill alive on the eighth.'

Dai Chippo licked his dry lips.

'If Evans didn't do it, who you after then?'

Crow glanced at Jones. Expressionlessly, the Inspector said, 'A man who fits a description, Dai. He'll be a man of few moral scruples, maybe one with a criminal record of some kind. He'll be a Welshman, and a Rhondda man, probably brought up in the valley. He'll have the sort of job where he can come and go as he pleases, with no one to ask where he's been at any particular time, so he could have come up the valley on several occasions from the end of May to the beginning of June.'

'All that's pretty general,' Dai Chippo said.

'We have some specifics too. He'd have to be a man who would have developed the sort of investigatory skills that would have allowed him, first, to trace Martin Evans when Donna came looking for him; second, to note the curious relationship existing between Evans and Ceinwen Williams and to ask a few questions about it; and third, to hit upon the idea of obtaining the truth from Lily Jenkins. To reach Lily Jenkins, he must have heard some whispers, long ago, about the fathering of Ceinwen, local whispers' private whispers, family whispers, and once he learned Evans's true identity, Lily could perhaps provide the key. And she did. So we want a local man with local knowledge, a greedy man who told Donna Stark her husband's new name but not his old secret, a vicious man who agreed to work with her when she returned in a hurry by taxi from the Rhondda on the sixth but murdered her when she threatened *him* on the eighth. A man who'd terrify an old woman in May, blackmail Evans in June, and murder Donna Stark the same month. Does that sum it up, sir?'

Crow nodded. 'Admirably.'

Slowly, Dai Chippo rose to his feet. He stood, shaking slightly, and his face was ashen. He stepped backwards and his clumsy movement sent the chair falling with a clatter, but in spite of the noise his gaze remained fixed on Teddy Skene.

'Bloody hell,' he said and scurried across the room towards the window as though fearful of contamination.

Skene ignored him, took out a cigarette, lit it casually. His hand was not shaking; he appeared perfectly calm.

'Was it an accident?' Crow asked him quietly. 'Or couldn't you face the threat of Donna clinging to your bank book the way she'd clung to Klein's, and wanted to cling to Evans's?'

Skene looked at Crow and shook his head.

'I don't know what you're talking about.'

'She wanted to drop Martin Evans, but she still wanted someone to hook on to. The someone was to be you. She was going to bleed you. . . you had to pay her, or she'd tell Martin you were the real blackmailer. And you knew just how much silence meant to Evans. So you killed her. You strangled her . . .'

'You'll never prove a thing,' Skene said in contempt.

* * *

'We'll prove it all right,' Crow said to Jason Warlock on the steps outside the Crown Court. 'It all links up: Donna's rush back on the sixth to beard Skene, his reluctant agreement to use her as an accomplice, his rage when she got scared and wanted to back out of blackmailing Evans only to turn her attention to him. We'll be having a second cousin of his to testify that there were rumours years ago that Ceinwen's father was Alan Stark. When Skene discovered Martin Evans was really Martin Stark and Ceinwen was working for him he did the pressure bit on Lily Jenkins. And that old lady will recognize him again, I'm sure of that. He made quite an impression on her as the man from the Council. Dewi Jones and the Chief Superintendent will make sure they have more proof this next time, anyway, with tighter caulking of the ship.'

'I hope so,' Warlock said, smiling, 'for the sake of the prosecution, and my client. Evans told me, by the way. . .she did try to blackmail him and he hit her. He'll testify to that.'

'What a mess,' Crow said tiredly, 'Klein is now unlikely to marry his heiress and is headed for bankruptcy; Dai Davies is in trouble with his wife.' He looked around at the elegant civic buildings, the distant clouds above

Cardiff Castle and the hint of green from Sophia Gardens. 'But worst of all, there's Ceinwen and Martin Evans.'

'Hmmm.' Warlock nodded thoughtfully. 'I've spoken to the Williams woman. A shy mouse; the publicity will crucify her. It's what Evans was trying to avoid, it's what sent him into a rage with Donna Stark, made him prepared to accept guilt for a crime he didn't commit. God knows he feels guilty inside: he's got a strong religious streak, as has the Williams woman. So Evans is suffering from moral guilt, social guilt, even guilt for her death, for if he hadn't failed Donna in their marriage, he feels, she wouldn't have died. Ceinwen and Martin . . . as you say, a mess, but it will blow over.'

'He'll be worried about his trial.'

Warlock looked surprised.

'I don't understand. What do you mean, trial? What on earth has Martin Evans now got to be worried about?'

Crow stared at the lawyer.

'Incest and bigamy! Hasn't he got enough to worry about?'

Warlock laughed and shook his head.

'Go back to your Moriarty, Chief Inspector Crow and leave the real law to us lawyers! Bigamy? The Marriage Act 1949 by its Schedule 1 sets out the prohibited degrees of consanguinity. It declares that a marriage celebrated between a half-brother and half-sister, whether the relationship is traced through wedlock or not, is *void.* It follows then that if Evan's marriage to Ceinwen was void—no marriage can be deemed to have taken place. It then follows that if the marriage cannot be said to have legally taken place, how can this second marriage be bigamous? It can't be—since his first marriage never took legal form, in effect.'

Warlock shook his head again, squinted up into the pale sunshine.

'And a charge of incest? The fact is, Evans has committed no crime. The Sexual Offences Act 1956, section 10, states it is a criminal offence for a man to have sexual intercourse with a woman he *knows* to be his half-sister. Martin Evans was not aware of the relationship any more than Ceinwen Williams was—until her grandmother disclosed the situation, after they had married. I tell you, man, they're both in the clear! There'll be no prosecution to face for either of them!'

* * *

Trust a lawyer to miss the point Crow thought as he walked alone towards Sophia Gardens in the sunshine. Know the law, ignore the reality. Muffled words struggled in his brain as he walked, words he had heard and not understood at the time, though coincidentally they would have given him a clue to the truth in the Evans case had they really registered at the time.

What were they?

That lecturer at the Conference in Cardiff, he had been speaking, answering a question just as Crow had decided to leave the hall. What was it he had said?

Moral responsibility . . . social responsibility . . . the Levitical injunction. . . the rigorous hostility of the Judaic-Christian ethic.

These were the things Martin and Ceinwen had to contend with, within the society in which they lived, and within themselves. The speaker's words came back to Crow, finally, as sadly he stared into the dark river water flowing towards the city.

'For them in this modern world, must life be a tragedy, must to love be a crime . . .?'

THE END

Thank you for reading this book. If you enjoyed it please leave feedback on Amazon, and if there is anything we missed or you have a question about then please get in touch. The author and publishing team appreciate your feedback and time reading this book.

Our email is office@joffebooks.com

www.joffebooks.com

INSPECTOR JOHN CROW SERIES

Book 1: A LOVER TOO MANY
Book 2: ERROR OF JUDGMENT
Book 3: THE WOODS MURDER
Book 4: MURDER FOR MONEY
Book 5: MURDER IN THE MINE

More Inspector John Crow books coming soon!
Join our mailing list to be the first to hear about them
www.joffebooks.com/contact/

22336294R00109

Printed in Great Britain
by Amazon